Search for

JUDAH'S GOLD

RALPH S. ORLANDELLA

This a work of fiction. Although characters take part in actual historical events, at actual locations, meeting real historical figures, many of the situations have been invented.

For My wife Paula
& Amanda and Adam

CONTENTS

ACKNOWLEDGMENTS

I would like to thank the California State Railroad Museum and Archives, especially Kyle Wyatt and Phil Sexton, both of whom have a wealth of knowledge on the building of the Central Pacific Railroad over California's Donner Pass.

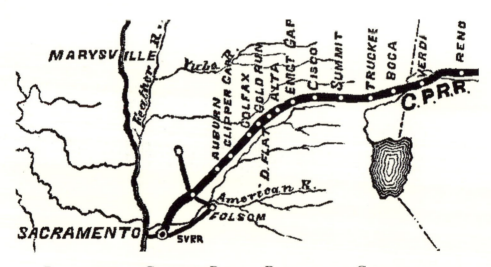

ROUTE OF THE CENTRAL PACIFIC RAILROAD IN CALIFORNIA

Gov. Stanford – The first locomotive
on the Central Pacific Railroad

Photo by California State Railroad Museum

CHAPTER ONE

Theodore Judah and the Big Four

Sacramento, California, October 1863

Walking down K Street toward the busy waterfront, Theodore Judah could not help but feel a sense of pride in his part in making Sacramento the heart of California. He looked at the paving stones beneath his feet and noted that even these "Folsom Potatoes" were transported by the Sacramento Valley Railroad, which he had built. Now his dream of building a transcontinental railroad was nearly a reality because of President Lincoln's signing the Pacific Railroad Act.

Judah stopped briefly and looked up the signboard on top of a two-story building. It read "Huntington Hopkins Hardware." He took a deep breath, entered a door at the far left of the next building, and climbed the staircase to the offices of the Central Pacific Railroad. He entered a formal meeting room with a long table surrounded by bearded men, and several clerical assistants were seated on the perimeter of the boardroom.

As Judah entered the room, a dark-bearded man briefly stood up and said, "Theodore, we have been waiting for you."

The man was Governor Leland Stanford. Judah thought about how the man's importance and connections in California had first led Judah to seek his support in the building of his railroad. Now it was these very connections that had become a complication to building the railroad. Leland Stanford had always been a strong supporter, but now his partners were influencing his judgment. Governor Stanford sat and continued speaking. "We understand you disagree with our handling of the Central Pacific Railroad."

Judah's face tightened in a grimace as he said, "There are a number of issues that must be addressed. First, I believe the board is attempting to defraud the United States government. You want me to report that Arcade Creek, just seven miles outside Sacramento, is the beginning of the Sierra Nevada mountain range, but the actual grade of the Sierra does not start for another twenty miles. Reporting in this manner would unfairly give the owners of the railroad an increased payment of six hundred and forty thousand dollars."

Stanford remained seated as he answered, "We have been through this before. We have provided a geological survey that clearly shows the rock from Arcade Creek has the characteristics of rock from a mountain range."

Judah quickly responded, "This is chicanery to misrepresent the truth. And there is another thing I take issue with: substandard materials and construction methods are being used to prepare the rail bed in violation of the Pacific Railroad Act."

The gray-bearded Collis Huntington spoke up from his place at the table. "We have been aware of your unwarranted claims for some time. Governor Stanford, Charles Crocker, Mark Hopkins and I have made arrangements to purchase your ownership."

Stanford looked at Judah and said, "Theodore, I have always had great respect for you and trust your work. The majority owners of this board have decided that it would be in the best interest of the railroad to purchase your stock in the company for one hundred thousand dollars and retain you as the Chief Engineer of the Central Pacific Railroad."

Judah's eyes blazed at Huntington as he said, "As the founder of this railroad, it is I who should be offered the opportunity to purchase *your* shares in the railroad."

Stanford responded, "Certainly, Theodore, the members of this board are honest and fair-dealing businessmen. To be fair, we have approved issuing you an option to purchase the four major investors' shares for one hundred thousand dollars per person."

Stanford then took the purchase option document and a bank draft and handed them to Judah. Rising from his chair, Judah said, "I reluctantly accept this payment for now, but I will return with full payment for the purchase of this railroad."

Stanford stood and shook his hand, and Judah left without looking at anyone else in the boardroom. He slowly walked down the staircase and returned to the busy streets of Sacramento, where his friend Daniel "Doc" Strong was waiting for him.

"Doc, the Associates have taken over our railroad."

As they walked, Theodore explained that they had purchased his shares in the railroad for a hundred thousand dollars. "I can still remember the day that you came to me with the your route over the Sierra. We made our surveys and wrote the Letters of Incorporation for the Central Pacific Railroad at your drug store in Dutch Flat. There is no one I trust more than you to safeguard this money." Judah told him that he would be sailing to New York that same day to get new backers to purchase the railroad. "This is our railroad, and I will not let them take it away from us."

Judah and Strong walked a short distance to the St. Charles Hotel and approached two men sitting in hotel lobby. One of the men was a young man dressed in working clothes, and the other was an old man wearing the worn garb of a miner. The younger man jumped up from his seat and asked, "How did the meeting go?"

Judah frowned and held up the bank draft and purchase option. "Lewis, it was a disaster. They paid me off."

The old miner asked, "How much did you get?"

"Jim, the amount is not important. Stanford let that scoundrel Huntington influence him. The associates paid me one hundred thousand dollars, and it will take at least an additional three hundred thousand dollars to buy them out, plus enough operating money to start building the first forty miles of the railroad."

The old miner replied, "The money to purchase the railroad is not a problem. Your miner brothers have already promised more than enough gold to purchase the railroad."

"Their investment is important, but I must still raise enough to fund the construction costs."

At that moment, a tall mustached gentleman entered the lobby and walked up to Jim.

"Hot damn, if it ain't Sam Clemens," Jim exclaimed.

"I don't believe my eyes—Jim Smiley, in the flesh. Are you still betting on those frogs at Angels Camp?"

"What in tarnation are you up to these days, Sam?"

"I have been writing for the San Francisco *Daily Morning Call,* and for unknown reasons the *Territorial Enterprise* in Virginia City has become interested in me reporting for them again as well. So I am traveling to Virginia City to talk to them about their poor judgment. I am very particular about the type of job I take. I don't want to work. That is why I became a newspaper reporter."

Jim introduced Sam to Judah, Doc Strong, and Lewis Clement. Sam immediately said, "Excuse my rudeness, but aren't you the fella they call 'Crazy Judah'?"

"Sadly, that is what lot of people have taken to calling me."

"Congratulations. I have been called a lot worse. I'm convinced you're on the right track. This country needs to be linked coast to coast, although you are going to have a hell of time making it happen."

Sam excused himself and said he had a stage to catch.

Doc Strong turned to Judah and asked what he planned to do. Judah held out the bank draft. "The first step is to cash this before Huntington and Crocker change their minds," he said. "You will have to keep the money in a safe place for me until I return from New York."

Jim said, "The miners' brotherhood will keep it safe with their own gold."

The four men walked a block to the Adams Company building, where Judah talked to the Wells Fargo Bank manager and gave him the bank draft. He informed the manager that he would like to cash the draft and be paid in fifty-dollar gold coins. The bank manager briefly paused, then said, "It will take a few days to get the coins from Kellogg Mint in San Francisco."

Judah signed the note and instructed the manager to make payment to Daniel Strong. The manager nodded in acknowledgement as he walked back to the teller's cage.

They went back to the St. Charles Hotel, and Judah went upstairs for his wife Anna and their luggage. They all walked together toward the waterfront. As they walked, Judah spoke to each of his companions. He gave Doc Strong the purchase option document and said, "Keep this away from the Associates."

He looked at Lewis. "Make certain you keep your position surveying for the railroad. You have a big future with the Central Pacific Railroad, my Canadian friend. You have proven to be an outstanding surveyor, and you have all the skills to be a great engineer."

Judah then turned toward the short old miner. "You and the miners have become my brothers, and I am certain you will safeguard our investment. I am leaving for New York today, and I am relying on all of you to keep our money safe until my return. Is this all right with all of you?"

Jim immediately responded with the local miner response, "Satisfactory!"

Both Doc and Lewis smiled and nodded in agreement. Judah and his wife Anna then walked to the dock and went up the gangway of the steamboat headed to San Francisco to transfer to the steamship *St. Louis*. Three days later, Doc and Jim returned to the bank in a freight wagon loaded with shotgun-toting miners from Murphy's Diggins. They loaded four canvas sacks of fifty-dollar gold coins on to the wagon and covered them with a tarp.

They left town, traveling on J Street toward the Sierra. When they reached Murphys the following day, they placed each bag of coins into a barrel and hid the four barrels with the miner's association treasury in an old Indian burial cave about a mile outside of town. That night they had a miner's "shindig" and enjoyed the libations provided until daybreak.

CHAPTER TWO

Gold Country

Murphys, California, September 1866

The weather was bitter cold, and the clouds of the year's first storm were gathering as Doc Strong's stagecoach reached Murphys. The main street of this mining boomtown was lined with an assortment of wooden storefronts and larger stone and brick buildings. It was quiet except for activity at the Miner's Hall.

Doc's stagecoach stopped at the Sperry Hotel. He immediately took his bag and went into the saloon for a shot of whiskey to warm him from the cold. A bald miner followed him into the bar. Doc turned and looked at him. "Great seeing you again, you old hard-rock miner!" he exclaimed.

Jim Smiley replied, "What brings you here to Murphy's Diggins?"

"Jim, as you know, Theodore died of Panama fever in New York before he could speak to the Vanderbilt organization about funding the railroad. I know you have kept the gold safe, but there is a new threat. The Associates believe that we plan to use the option to purchase their interest in the railroad. Lewis Clement got word to me that Huntington and Crocker know we have the gold hidden here in Murphys. They have hired Pinkerton detectives to find the gold and get the purchase option document. The really bad news is, the four detectives are only a few hours behind me."

Jim asked, "Where can we hide the gold where it would be safer than here?"

Doc told the old miner, "Lewis has a special place to hide it, right under the Associates' noses."

Nearby, in Angels Camp, four horsemen rode into town and left their horses at the stable. The leader told the others, "Let's get a night's rest at the Angels Hotel. The weather is terrible, and the miners won't be able to move anything tonight anyway. We'll get an early start in the morning."

At Murphys, a miner rode in out of the night. He went straight to Jim Smiley and told him that four armed riders were in Angels Camp and had asked for the fastest route to Murphys. The excited miner added that he thought they were after the miner's' gold hoard. Jim thanked him and said, "We had better get moving."

The miners quickly hijacked two freight wagons and brought them to the miner's' "Hall of Comparative Ovations," where several armed miners climbed aboard. They started down the muddy street, turning off between the Traver Building and the Jones Apothecary onto Sheep Ranch Mine Road. They traveled this road for about a mile, then turned off the road and went a short distance to a small wooden storage shed.

Several of the miners pushed the shed aside, and Doc could see the shed had hidden the opening of a cave. The mouth of the cave had a sharp drop into a cavern below. The miners dropped a rope into the opening and lowered a man to floor of the cavern below.

The miners had hidden their gold hoard and Judah's gold coins in twelve whiskey casks in a small chamber of the cavern. They carefully hoisted each barrel out of the cave, placed them on the wagon, and coved them with a tarp. Jim winked at Doc and said, "Nobody is crazy enough to try to take whiskey away from a miner."

Jim and Doc boarded the wagon, along with two miner guards carrying shotguns, and their wagon quickly clattered off into the dark, rainy night. On the ride to Murphys, Doc explained his plan to hide the gold.

During the past three years, Lewis Clement had been in charge of crews building the highest and most difficult portion of the Central Pacific Railroad. During that time, he designed the perfect hiding place for Judah's gold within sight of the railroad. His crew of Chinese workers had constructed a vault of solid granite, stronger than steel. It was totally out of sight of anyone looking for it.

While Jim and Doc were driving toward Murphys, four horsemen arrived at the Miner's' Hall in Murphys. They dismounted and opened the front door of the 'hall, where they found a lone miner, sleeping off a night of revelry in a corner of the bar.

The leader of the detectives gave him a nudge and by reflex the man hid his bottle of whiskey. The leader said, "My name is John Richardson and I work for the Pinkerton Detective Agency."

"We are looking for several men that have gold taken from the Central Pacific Railroad. They've hidden it here in Murphys."

He stared intently at the man and asked, Where do the miners keep their gold?" The terrified miner replied, "In the Wells Fargo Bank, in Columbia."

"Nice try, old man. Where do you keep it here in Murphys?"

"You might try looking in the pokey, right off Main Street. It's the safest place in town."

One of the detectives grabbed the miner by the scruff of the neck and told him to lead them to the jail. They walked a short distance to a small jailhouse. The iron doors were locked, but the detective easily opened them with a single bullet. The two cells inside the jail were empty. Richardson turned to the miner and said, "You're holding back, old man.

The miner took a swig from his bottle and said, "There is one other place where the gold could be hidden. There was a lot of activity there last night."

He led them for about a mile to a small wooden shed. The detectives opened the door and saw nothing but a coil of rope. The miner told them to move the shed aside. The four men slid the shed a few feet and exposed the cave's opening. They quickly dropped the rope into the opening and lowered Richardson into the cavern below. A few minutes later, he yelled up that there were fresh footprints in the dust, so they must have just been there and moved the gold. After pulling Richardson up out of the cave, he bellowed at he miner, "Where did they go?"

The miner replied, "There was a lot of commotion here last night, and when it quieted down, I saw a wagon headed on the trail toward Columbia."

A few miles away, the miner's wagon carefully rumbled down an old trail and crossed the river. Just before daybreak, the wagon climbed to the top of a very steep hill. As the wagon creaked to a stop, a mustached miner came out of a small wooden cabin and shouted, "What the hell is going on? Can't a man get a good night sleep?"

As he reached the wagon, he recognized Jim Smiley. "What the hell are you doing here in the middle of the night, you old claim jumper?"

"Sam, that's not a very neighborly greeting for a friend." Jim told Clemons that railroad detectives were trying to steal Judah's grubstake. Sam said, "I wondered what happened to all Judah's gold."

Doc explained to Sam that they had kept it safe in Murphys since Judah's death, but now they needed to hide it somewhere else.

Sam shook his head. "With all the places you could hide, why did you come to my diggins?"

Doc said, "We trust you, Sam, and Jackass Hill gives us an overview of countryside to watch for the Pinkerton men. Once they leave the area, it will be safe to move the gold."

At sunrise, Doc could see four riders through his field glasses, headed from Murphys in the direction of Jackass Hill. Sam smiled and said, "Have you thought about the fact that you are at the top of a hill, and there is nowhere to run?

The four riders turned off in the direction of Columbia.

"We told all the miners in Murphys to tell them we were headed to Columbia," Doc explained.

"It's time to go," Jim said." "They'll be searching the streets of Columbia all day before they figure out we aren't there. We should be in Sutter's Creek with a full day's lead by the time they discover their mistake." As they wagon started down the steep hill, he thanked Sam for his hospitality and raised his clenched fist in a miner's salute.

After two days of travel, which included repairing a broken wagon wheel, they reached the railroad in Colfax. They could see two small steam locomotives shuttling rails and railroad ties toward the railhead above. The names painted on the cabs of steamers were *C. P. Huntington* and *T. D. Judah.* Doc could not help but think of the irony of those locomotives being there.

T D Judah Locomotive
Photo by California State Railroad Museum

C P Huntington Locomotive at Alta California

Photo by California State Railroad Museum

The wagon headed toward a large canvas tent. Before they reached it, a young man rode out to meet them. Doc recognized Lewis Clement and greeted him and then said, "I was not certain that you were going to get here. The men they sent after you are some of Pinkerton's best men."

"Doc, everything is ready. We will move your cargo to the empty flat car and climb aboard for the trip to the railhead at Alta. My construction crew will meet us there."

"Hopefully, it will look like any other day on the railroad."

After the wagon was unloaded, Jim tossed a poke of gold dust to the miners on the wagon and said, "Boys, if you like, you can take the wagon to Sacramento and have a good time."

They immediately responded "Satisfactory!" The wagon slowly turned and headed down the trail, and they disappeared into the night. Lewis said, "You can make camp here tonight, and we will start climbing in the morning."

Early the next morning, they had breakfast in the railroad camp; and after the railroad car was loaded, they climbed aboard. One of Lewis's crew ran up and told him he could see riders approaching from below the camp.

A few minutes later, the diminutive *C. P. Huntington* gave two long blasts from its whistle and slowly started the three-mile climb up to Cape Horn. When the train rounded Cape Horn, they could see the American River Canyon almost two thousand feet below the rail. About an hour later, they reached the railhead at Alta.

As they unloaded the barrels, Lewis told his companions, "If you look about a quarter mile down the track, you will see a tent. It belongs to my boss, Samuel Montague. Montague was a close friend of Judah's and replaced him as the railroad's chief engineer when he died. A few feet off the railroad right of way, you will see a cabin that belongs to Crocker's superintendent of construction, James Strobridge." "Don't worry, though; Montague will delay Strobridge or any other of the Associate's' men who try to follow us."

Lewis saddled his favorite roan mule and brought two more saddled mules out the corral for Doc and Jim. He told them, "The mules are more sure-footed than horses on the rocky route ahead." Lewis's Chinese crew loaded two barrels on each pack mule and each led a string of three mules. The weather was excellent except for occasional strong gusts of wind, and the group traveled rapidly all day along the railroad grade. They reached Cisco at nightfall and made camp near the Tunnel 3 construction camp.

In the morning, one of Lewis's workers told him they could see several horsemen riding along the riverbed in the canyon below. Lewis immediately went to the crew foreman and asked if was going to do any blasting in Tunnel 3 today. The foreman replied that he had a full day of blasting planned.

"Great, see those riders along the river?" Lewis explained that the horsemen would be climbing up to Cisco this morning, and he wanted him to delay them all day.

The foreman smiled and said, "I plan on blasting all day and night on both Tunnel 3 and Tunnel 4. It will not be safe for anyone to pass after you leave."

Lewis thanked him and quickly got Doc, Jim, and the pack mules moving. "Hurry up, Jim; it's going to get very noisy here."

The mules moved slowly along the treacherous mountainside as they made their way around Big Bend. They could hear the sound of blasting echoing along the mountainside. The weather suddenly changed to a combination of rain and snow; at one point, one of the mules almost lost its footing. The sky cleared just as they planned to stop for the night, and a full moon was visible. Lewis said, "We are almost there; let's keep traveling. There is no way that the Pinkerton men could ride horses on this route, even if they managed to get past my crew."

Finally, they reached a valley, where they stopped briefly at Mineral Spring House. They then traveled up to the crest of the mountain. Lewis directed them a few hundred feet away to a cave-like opening in the top of the granite mountain pass.

The Chinese crew unloaded the cargo from the mules and lowered the barrels about twenty feet down into a vault-like opening cut out of solid granite. After the last of the barrels was placed in the vault, a huge granite door was pivoted into place, sealing the precious cargo inside the mountain. Daniel said, "Lewis, you and your men did great work. Now that the entrance is sealed, no one looking at this would ever find the opening."

The last worker out of the cave gave Lewis two metal objects. Lewis handed them to Doc and said, "These are the keys to unlock the granite door. They must be used together to open the vault. When they are in place, the lock can be opened like a Chinese puzzle box." Doc kept one of the objects and gave the other to Jim, telling him, "Keep this safe or we will never be able to retrieve the gold."

Lewis said, "We had better split up. I will take my crew east to the next camp. Doc knows his way home from here, so, Jim, you stay with him and head to Dutch Flat. Make sure you stay clear of the detectives." Doc thanked Lewis, and he and Jim headed west.

CHAPTER THREE

The New Generation

*August 1958, Onboard Train 98, the Coast Daylight,
South of Santa Barbara*

Looking out of the window of the tavern car, Dan Strong could see four coastal islands in the distance. He took a seat in a semicircular booth so he could continue to enjoy the ever-changing view of the California coastline. He had barely settled in his seat when a white-uniformed waiter asked if would like a drink. "A cold Coca Cola with no ice," he ordered, and asked for a ham sandwich from the diner.

The waiter smiled and said, "I will be right back."

Dan had chosen to travel on the *Coast Daylight* because he enjoyed the laid-back atmosphere and excellent service that was a railroad tradition. He traveled by air only when absolutely necessary. He had recently returned from archeology dig in Egypt by ocean liner, and when he reached New York, he boarded the *20th Century Limited* to Chicago. From there, he then enjoyed traveling on the fabulous vista-domed railroad cars of the *California Zephyr* back to his home in Sacramento. Flying would have saved days of travel, but he enjoyed his time on the train. It was his private time to clear his mind and reenergize.

After a few minutes, the waiter returned with his sandwich and a small glass bottle of Coca-Cola and asked if he would like a glass. When Dan nodded, the waiter poured the contents of the bottle into a glass and gave him the bill. Dan looked at the receipt and paid the tab, adding a generous tip for the waiter.

As Dan began eating his sandwich, a tall, attractive, raven-haired woman walked up to the booth and asked, "May I join you, Professor Strong?"

He looked at the young woman and said, "Of course, you may join me." She placed her drink on the table and gracefully slid into the booth. Dan noticed the woman was wearing a dark designer dress, and her jewelry clearly had been purchased at Tiffany's.

"My name is Veronica Bailey. Please excuse me for intruding, but I recognized you from a lecture I attended at Stanford University. You were discussing your recent archeological discoveries in Capri and Egypt. I tried to enroll in your class, but I was told you were on sabbatical."

"I am getting ready to conduct some field studies here in California," he told her, "and I am traveling to Los Angeles to speak to the California Historical Society. After that, I will be working with my research partner to develop our schedule."

"I am curious how you managed to find the golden wreath crown of Tiberius Caesar and his treasure, when so many archeologists before you had studied the Villa of Jupiter and failed to find it," she said.

Dan laughed. "It was dumb luck. We were finishing a dig at the Villa of Jupiter for the University when my associate dropped a folder with all our team's research results over a cliff below the Palace of Tiberius. We could see the results of our research on a small outcropping of rock about halfway down the cliff."

Dan explained that the Villa of Jupiter, or Villa Jovis, is located atop the second highest peak on Capri with a spectacular view of the Gulf of Naples. The notes were dropped off "Tiberius's Lcap," where, according to legend, Tiberius hurled disobedient servants and unwelcome guests to their deaths.

"My students found several hundred feet of rope, which they attached to the bottom of a column. They then ran the rope through a pulley and tied it to my waist and lowered me about two hundred feet to the rock outcrop, and I grabbed the notes. Before they hauled me back to the top, I noticed a small opening in the cliff and the glint of metal shining from inside. After digging with my hands to enlarge the opening, I pulled out a golden laurel leaf wreath and a golden ring with the seal of Tiberius Caesar. During the next few weeks, we retrieved the rest of Tiberius's treasure and documented the find."

Dan gave a brief background history on the find. During his reign, Tiberius became reclusive and feared that he might be killed. He hid all his symbols of power in the cliff to keep them out of the hands of rivals. His fears came true when Caligula and the leader of the Praetorian Guard smothered him with his own pillow.

Dan glanced out the window. He could see the train had reached Ventura and started its turn inland, away from the ocean view he had enjoyed for the last hundred miles. He turned and looked at Veronica.

"Why is an elegant woman like you so interested in a down-to-earth, dirty profession like archeology?" he asked.

"Archeology has always fascinated me, ever since I first heard about Howard Carter's discovery of King Tut's tomb in the Valley of the Kings. But honestly, my main interest is the history of California. I have strong ties to California's gold rush. My great-grandfather, James Bailey, was a successful jeweler in Sacramento during the gold rush years."

Dan interrupted, "Was your great-grandfather the same James Bailey that invested in the Central Pacific Railroad?"

"Yes, he was one of the first investors in Theodore Judah's crazy dream to build a transcontinental railroad over the Sierra. My great-grandfather's stories were passed down from generation to generation, along with a few souvenirs from that time. Because of this, I have always been interested in the sites and history of the Central Pacific Railroad."

Dan told Veronica that his research partner and he had similar backgrounds. "Both our great-grandfathers worked with Theodore Judah, carrying on surveys of the Sierra Nevada mountains, searching for the best route for a transcontinental railroad."

Veronica smiled. "Your research partner is Katherine Kelly," she said. "I have read about her in reviews of your archeology projects in Capri and the Egyptian desert. I get the impression you two are very close."

Dan blushed slightly. "We have been friends since were kids. Our families have kept a close relationship for generations and, yes, we have a serious personal relationship."

"I recently heard your next research project would focus on the building of the Central Pacific Railroad and finding Judah's gold," Veronica went on.

Dan's face tightened as he said, "Whoa! How do you know about Judah's gold?"

"My great-grandfather was in the boardroom when the Associates paid Judah one hundred thousand dollars for his interest in the Central Pacific Railroad. He was also the man that Charles Crocker asked to find and retrieve Judah's option-to-purchase document that had been signed by Leland Stanford."

Dan studied Veronica. "He was also after Judah's one hundred thousand dollars."

She quickly replied, "James Bailey and the Big Four did not care about Judah's money; they only wanted to buy back the option to purchase the railroad. They were afraid Judah's friends would find the financial backing to buy back the railroad at a bargain price, just when they were starting to get payments and land grants from the federal government. When they were not successful in getting the document, they shielded the Central Pacific Railroad under the corporate umbrella of the Southern Pacific Railroad that they acquired."

The orange and red railroad passenger cars of the *Coast Daylight* curved through the Chatsworth Rocks and Santa

Susana Pass, then started the decent into the San Fernando Valley below.

"Veronica, it sounds like it is not a coincidence that we crossed paths on this train. What is it that you want?"

"Even though the Bailey family amassed a fortune and has lived in San Francisco luxury, we have not forgotten our roots in Sacramento. I want to find both Judah's gold and the miners' gold hidden with it. I have no noble intentions; I want it for my personal collection. I am willing to fund your search and divide the gold evenly."

"Miss Bailey, I am not in this profession for the money," Dan replied. "History and archeology are my life. If anything of historical value is found, it will belong to the public. And I am not in need of any financial support for my work. Thank you for your interest, but my answer is no."

"You can't fault a lady for making a direct approach," she said, with a smile. "Now I will just have to find it before you do. I am disappointed that we will not be working together on this project, but I will be putting all my resources into finding Judah's gold.

"Goodbye, Dr. Strong. I am truly disappointed we will not have a chance to work together."

She smiled at Dan and walked toward the rear of the train.

LOS ANGELES UNION PASSENGER TERMINAL

PHOTO BY BA'GAMNAN

CHAPTER FOUR

Los Angeles Union Station

Dan looked out of the window. He could see the train was stopped at the Glendale train station, and when the train left the station Dan decided he should walk a few cars forward so he could exit the train quickly when it reached the next station. As he walked, he could see Mission Tower at the entrance of Los Angeles Union Passenger Terminal. He reached the vestibule of his car as the *Coast Daylight* arrived on Track 7. In a matter of seconds, the railroad porter had opened the vestibule door and lifted the metal deck, dropping the steps into place. The porter grabbed an orange step and placed on the platform then everyone to Los Angeles.

Dan put on his favorite Boston Red Sox baseball cap and descended the steps he was immediately bear-hug and kissed by young attractive red-haired woman. "I missed you, Dan," she exclaimed.

"Geesh, Kate, it's only been a few days."

Dan gave his baggage tag to a redcap, who pulled a suitcase and briefcase out of the baggage elevator. Dan gave him a tip and thanked him, then walked with Kate down the ramp to the terminal. As they walked Dan told Kate that he was really looking forward to spending time with her in Hollywood and he had a surprise for her.

Veronica Bailey approached them, followed by a redcap pushing her luggage on a cart. "Nice talking to you, Dan. I am certain we will cross paths again in the near future."

Dan and Kate watched Veronica go through a station patio to the taxi area and get into a waiting limousine. As they walked past the Harvey House Restaurant to the massive Union Station waiting room, Kate turned to Dan and asked, "Who was that woman?"

"She's trouble. I'll fill you in later."

They found Kate's red 1956 Ford Thunderbird in the parking lot, and as they drove off Dan said, "I got an early start, and the only thing I ate today was a ham sandwich." "Why don't we drive a couple blocks up Alameda to Philippe's? I'm craving a French dip sandwich and lemonade."

Kate rolled her eyes, but did as he suggested and parked in front of the restaurant. "Don't you ever get tired of eating here?" she asked.

"Never! The only thing tastier is a Fenway Frank at a Red Sox game."

They walked into the diner, went over to the "carver" at the deli station, and ordered two French dip sandwiches and lemonades. The man quickly prepared their order and handed it to them over the counter. They sat down at a window table, and Kate said, "Okay, Dan, who was that woman at the station?"

"Like I said, Kate, she is going to be major trouble when we start our next project. Veronica Bailey is related to one of the Central Pacific board members that bought Judah out in 1863. She knows about Judah's gold and the miner's' gold hoard and wants to add it to her collection. She is a treasure hunter and has the finances to make it happen."

Kate asked, "How could she find it without our artifacts?"

Dan replied, "Bailey needs access to all of the artifacts to complete the puzzle. We must be extremely careful, because she will attempt to follow us and steal the puzzle pieces."

"How did you meet her?"

Dan explained that Veronica had introduced herself to him on the train and immediately started working him for information. "She already knew about Judah's option-to-purchase document, and she also knew we have items that can lead us to the gold. She even offered to finance the project and have a partnership with a 50/50 split," he said.

Kate dipped her sandwich in the au jus and said, "That bitch is dangerous."

"Kate, in the future, we cannot let the documents and artifacts out of our sight. I have my items in my brief case. Where are you keeping the watch and Judah's surveyor's plumb bob?"

Kate pulled a gold pocket watch and chain out of her handbag, saying, "It's my constant companion."

She also pulled out a small metal top-shaped item out of her purse and gave it to Dan. He looked at it closely and said, "This is a surveyor's plumb bob, and it is engraved 'T Judah'."

Dan took a metal spike out of his briefcase and showed it to Kate. It looked like a railroad spike, with an unusual triangle-shaped point and the number 1053 stamped into the head. He explained that he had seen spikes like this used by surveyors as monument markers in rocky terrain. He placed both of the artifacts in a small leather bag and said, "These were handed down by our families, and we have always been told that they are keys to the hiding place of Judah's gold."

Dan then opened his briefcase and carefully pulled two documents out of an archival acid-free envelope. The first document was the option to purchase Stanford, Huntington, Hopkins, and Crocker's shares in the Central Pacific for one hundred thousand dollars per person. The certificate was issued to Theodore Judah or his designee. The second document was a Wells Fargo Bank receipt from 1863, documenting the payment of one hundred thousand dollars in gold coins from Theodore Judah to Daniel Strong.

Dan placed a brown coin envelope on the table and pulled out a heavy fifty-dollar gold coin. Dan explained, "This is an 1855 gold coin, minted in San Francisco by the Kellogg private mint because the newly opened San Francisco U.S. Mint could not keep up with the demand for gold coins. It is extremely rare, and only eleven or twelve are known to exist. Doc Strong was paid with two thousand of these 2½ ounce gold coins by the Wells Fargo Bank. He kept one of the coins with his diary to prove that the gold exists."

Dan told Kate that he would go public on the documents at the Historical Society meeting. "Veronica Bailey most likely knows about them, because her great-grandfather James Bailey was in the boardroom when they were given to Judah," he said. "I will not release any information on your watch or the other items that were passed down to us.

"We also must do a background search on my new friend Veronica Bailey. She appears to know everything about us and we know nothing about her. We'll have to pay a visit to our FBI friend Jack Packard after the conference."

They finished their meal and walked to the car. Kate took the wheel and said, "We are off to the Roosevelt."

There was very little traffic as that evening as they traveled to Hollywood. They drove by Grauman's Chinese Theater and could see the bright red neon "Hotel Roosevelt" sign a block away. Kate turned into the rear entrance of the hotel, and a valet took her keys and gave her a claim tag.

Dan and Kate entered the hotel lobby then walked up the staircase to the mezzanine level. Kate had arranged for two adjacent Cabana suites over the pool and Tropicana bar. Dan opened his door and looked at Kate.

"Kate, do you want to go down to the pool bar for a drink?"

"Sure!" she responded.

Dan placed his suitcase in the room and, after making certain the door was locked, went downstairs with Kate and sat at a poolside table. The server took their orders; Kate ordered a Planter's Punch, and Dan ordered a rum and Coke.

A poolside party was in full swing at the bar area, with quite a number of celebrities joining in. One of them even looked like Marilyn Monroe. Kate said, "I heard that the hotel was not drawing people like it did at the peak of the Hollywood era, but it sure looks like quite a party tonight."

"Kate, this venerable old hotel has a history people don't want to forget," Dan replied. "I'm really pleased the Historical Society picked it for their convention site."

The waitress returned with their drinks. Kate noticed Dan still had his briefcase and pointed to it. "You talked about playing it safe; should we put the artifacts in the hotel safe?"

Dan squinted and said, "No way! They stay with us at all times."

"Dan, you really think that mysterious woman is going to make an attempt to steal them?"

"I know her type. Veronica Bailey probably has already hired some goons to get them."

They finished their drinks, and Dan told Kate they needed to get some rest, as the following day would be very busy. Kate frowned. "It's still early, and the party looks like a lot of fun."

Dan stood up and reached his hand out to her. Together they made their way through the poolside crowd. When they reached Kate's door, she turned to him and asked, "Don't you want to come in for a while, Dan?" Dan said, "Don't tempt me, sweetheart, we have a big day ahead of us."

"Good night, Kate. We need to get some rest."

CHAPTER FIVE

The Roosevelt

When they met in the lobby the next morning, Dan asked Kate if she would like to have a late breakfast at Musso and Frank. She smiled and said, "That sounds like a great way to start the day. What time is your keynote speech?"

Dan told her it was scheduled for 1:00 p.m., after lunch. "I am really going to have to make it interesting to keep them awake."

They walked to the north entrance of the hotel, and Dan held the door open for a blonde in a cocktail dress who had just waked out of the Cinegrill. As she walked through the door, she looked at Kate.

"You have quite a gentleman. You better keep a close eye on this looker, or someone may try to steal him away from you."

Dan and Kate's eyes opened wide as they realized that the blonde was Marilyn Monroe. Marilyn said to Dan, "Could you be a real sweetie and hail a cab for me? I have to get to my bungalow at the Beverly Hills Hotel."

Dan promptly hailed a cab at the curb and said, "Here you go, Marilyn."

Marilyn gave Dan her card and said, "You kids look like might enjoy watching my next movie being filmed. Show this card to the guard on at the Goldwyn Studio on the fourth, and he'll give you directions to my soundstage."

Marilyn blew Dan a kiss and climbed into the backseat of the cab, and Dan closed the door. She waved as she drove off down Hollywood Boulevard.

As the cab drove off, Kate said, "What a way to start your day!"

Dan shook his head in disbelief, as Kate took his hand and said, "Okay, Romeo, let's go have some breakfast."

They walked down Hollywood Boulevard, past the Paramount Theater and Grauman's Theater, to the Musso and Frank Restaurant. As they entered the restaurant, a red-jacketed waiter whisked them off to a large, mahogany booth with deep red leather upholstery. They both ordered flannel cakes with bacon, potatoes, and coffee. The waiter returned with their coffee, and Dan asked to see Kate's gold pocket watch again. She told him, "It still keeps perfect time, even after nearly a century of use." She handed Dan the watch, and he took a close look at the engraving on the back. The watch was beautifully engraved by hand.

Jim Smiley,
Supreme Noble Humbug,
Murphy's Diggins

The edge of the watchcase was also engraved, with letter that looked like primary directions on a compass and a small arrow pointing east.

Dan noticed a small gold key at the end of the watch chain. "Do you know what this key opens?" he asked.

Kate told him it opened Jim Smiley's ornately carved wooden cigar box. She said she had snatched it as a kid and had always used it to hide letters and other favorite things. Dan told her he would like to take a look at it when they got home. Dan then said, "I would like to have a jeweler has done restoration work for me look at the watch and service it for you tomorrow, so it keeps running for the next hundred years."

The waiter placed their breakfast and hot maple syrup in front of them, saying, "Enjoy your breakfast."

They both devoured the ultrathin pancakes and crisp bacon and walked back to the Roosevelt a few minutes later. When they reached their rooms, they both could see that they had had a visitor while they were gone. The rooms were tossed upside down by someone searching the room. Dan replied," We must have had a visit by some of Bailey's men. Fortunately, there was nothing for them to find. You have the watch, and everything else is in my briefcase."

Kate and Dan returned to the hotel lobby, which was milling with people attending the convention. Dan walked up to the counter and told the desk clerk, "I would like to report a break-in in our two suites."

The hotel manager was immediately called to the counter, and he asked them for their names. Dan responded, "We are Daniel Strong and Katherine Kelly." "That is very strange. A gentleman just came to the counter and used your name and asked to remove his valuables from the hotel safe. He even had a driver's license with your name. Of course, he did not get anything, as you have not left any valuables with us."

The manager picked up the phone and called hotel security and the housekeeping department. Within a minute, they could see four housekeepers hurrying up to their rooms. The manager told Kate and Dan he was extremely sorry about break-in and asked if there was anything he else he could do for them. Dan turned to Kate. "Why don't you go up to the room and get ready when they finish cleaning up? I will be there in a few minutes to change into my suit for the presentation."

He then moved to the side of the counter and had a private conversation with the hotel manager. Dan then went back to his room and could see the room was immaculate and everything had been returned to its proper place. He quickly changed into a business suit and there was a knock on the door and he heard Kate say, "We are going to be late."

Dan opened the door. Kate had her hair up and had changed into attractive business attire. "You look fantastic, Kate. Let's head down to the ballroom for the meeting." Kate replied, You look very dashing as well—like a young Cary Grant."

Dan and Kate walked down to the Blossom Ballroom, where they saw over two hundred people seated classroom-style in the room. They walked to the front presenter's table. Dan seated Kate and said, "I will be right back; there is something I have to check on."

Dan returned to the table a few minutes later and sate down beside with a mischievous smile on his face. Kate asked, "What's up?"

Dan raised his finger to his lips. "You'll find out during my presentation."

The President of the California Historical Society went to the microphone on the podium and welcomed the historians to the Society's annual conference. He said, "I know you have all been busy at your special-interest breakout meetings this morning. I feel fortunate to have our speaker Dr. Daniel T. Strong and his associate Dr. Katherine S. Kelly with us today. They are both archeologists and historians on the Stanford University faculty who have been very busy in Italy and Egypt during the past few years. Their recent archeological digs resulted in two fabulous historical finds, the golden crown and treasure of Tiberius Caesar in Italy and the discovery of a royal cache of Pharaoh's treasure in Egypt. Their next major project will focus on the history, planning, and building of the first transcontinental railroad here in California. At this time, I would like turn the microphone over to Dr. Strong."

Dan walked to the microphone at the podium, thanked the host for the introduction, and then started his presentation.

"You have to be wondering what two archeologists fresh from digs in Capri and Egypt are doing addressing the premier scholars of California History. My associate Dr. Kelly and I are both third-generation Californians descended from men who assisted Theodore Judah on engineering surveys of the Sierra, determining the best route for the Central Pacific Railroad. Both of us have had family history of that time passed down from generation to generation. This information is key to understanding the events that occurred during the building of the Central Pacific Railroad that have been missed by the historical record.

"During our graduate studies, we wrote extensively on the events in California history, and we agreed that one day we would focus on researching the people, sites, and events that resulted in the building of a railroad through an almost impassible mountain range. Stanford University was so impressed with our graduate work that they offered us both positions as professors in classical archeology and funded digs in Italy and Egypt. Now that we have returned, they are allowing us to develop a project of our own; so, with the full backing of the University, we have a full team of graduate students and the resources to conduct our next research studies in California's Sierra Nevada Mountains.

"As you have already heard, the focus of the study project will be researching significant events that occurred during the building of the Central Pacific Railroad and validating the documents and artifacts that Dr. Kelly's family and my family passed down to us. Later in this presentation, I will be sharing information that will open a new historical window on California. Before I do this, I would like to explain our philosophy on pursuing archeological research and validating significant events in history.

"Dr. Kelly and I are not treasure hunters. We have been fortunate to discover priceless artifacts during our first two projects. Our reward has always been finding the missing pages of history. The treasure that we find is priceless because of the story it tells. These items belong to the people of the lands they came from and never should become the trophies of a collector. You are all historians, and I am certain you did not enter your profession to get rich. You became historians to learn from the past and to ensure this information is passed on to future generations. This is why you are teachers communicating the past to the students who are our future.

"Now I am going to tell you about our new project. I am certain that you know the story of Theodore Judah and his disagreements with the 'Associates,' better known as the 'Big Four' of the Central Pacific Railroad. I have firsthand information on the details of that time, recorded in the diary of my great-grandfather. It fills in the missing pages of the history of the building of the first transcontinental railroad. As you may have already deduced, my great-grandfather was Doc Strong, the Dutch Flat druggist who showed Judah the future route of the Central Pacific Railroad through the treacherous peaks of the Sierra Nevada mountain range. He was also Judah's first partner in the Central Pacific Railroad Corporation they founded in 1860.

"I have a question for the audience. What did the directors of the Central Pacific Railroad do to make Judah travel to New York to find new backers for his railroad?"

Several people in the audience raised their hands, and Dan pointed to a young man in the second row. The man stood up and said, "The Associates bought out his shares of the railroad corporation because of his disagreement with the way they were managing the railroad."

Dan said, "That is correct. Do you know how much they paid him, and what happened to the money?"

The young man replied, "I believe they paid him one hundred thousand dollars, and I have no idea what happened to the money."

"You are correct with both answers. He was paid one hundred thousand dollars, and the current pages of history do not tell what happened to the money. Today, I will reveal two documents and an artifact that will start to answer the question of what happened to the money. I will have them on display in a showcase in the lobby when my presentation is finished. The first document is an option to purchase the Central Pacific Railroad, which was issued to Theodore Judah or his designee. Leland Stanford, the president of the Central Pacific Railroad, signed this document.

"The second document is a Wells Fargo Bank receipt from October 1863 that documents the transfer of one hundred thousand dollars in gold coins from Judah's account to Daniel Strong. Daniel Strong's signature is on this document.

"The third item in the case is an extremely rare fifty-dollar gold coin minted in San Francisco in 1855. This coin has been certified as a genuine coin minted by the Kellogg private mint."

At this point, Dan could hear an increased murmur of conversation from the normally quiet audience.

"I can tell you that Doc Strong wrote in his journal that the gold was kept in a safe place until new investors were found to build the railroad. He kept one coin with the journal to validate his story. I can also tell you that my family has not looked for the gold, and it is still hidden in an unknown location in the Sierra.

"You now understand Dr. Kelly's and my interest in researching this unknown page of California history. I have just about used up my allotted time, and I would like to open it up for questions. I believe I only have enough time for a couple of questions, but Dr. Kelly and I will be available in the lobby for additional questions after this presentation.

"The documents and gold coin will be on display for an hour, and then they will be transported to Stanford University and stored with the Central Pacific Railroad's golden spike until an appropriate display location is determined."

Dan looked out at the audience, and an older gentleman immediately stood up and asked, "During my research in the mother lode area, I uncovered folk tales about Judah's gold. The stories are always tied to an E Clampus Vitus treasure of gold dust and gold nuggets. Do you have any information that might validate that myth?"

Dan heard the sounds of loud laughter coming from the audience and said, "Whenever E Clampus Vitus, or the 'Clampers,' are mentioned, some historians automatically write them off as a drunken group of wild miners. While drunken revelry is definitely part of the Clamper heritage, after an in-depth study of the California gold rush era, you will realize they did make a major impact on the mining communities throughout California. Dr. Kelly has documentation that there actually was a connection between Judah and the lost E Clampus Vitus treasury. Her great-grandfather Jim Smiley was a miner and member of the E Clampus brotherhood in Murphys and Angels Camp. Jim Smiley assisted Judah on most of his surveys for the Sacramento Valley Railroad and the Central Pacific Railroad.

"Miners and prospectors were the majority of Northern California's population during the gold rush. They were considered too rowdy to become members of fraternal organizations like the Masons or Odd Fellows, so they developed their own fraternal organization and called it the Brotherhood of E Clampus Vitus. The Clampers were such a strong part of the mining community that in order to do business in the mining community, you had to be invited to join the brotherhood. When a new member was initiated into the organization, the admission fee was generally a poke of gold dust. Over time, the Clampers built up a very large treasury."

"The Clampers were by far the largest benevolent organization in the mining communities of California. Their creed was 'Always look out for *widders* and orphans'. On numerous occasions, they bankrolled the rebuilding of entire towns after they were burned down by the fires that were common at the time. Information that Dr. Kelly and I have indicates that the Clampers did invest part of their treasury with Theodore Judah to help purchase the Central Pacific Railroad.

"Now, I can take one more question."

A tall, dark-haired woman in the rear of the room asked, "Do you have any other documents or artifacts that will be used during your research project?"

"Yes; as I previously hinted, we have Doc Strong's journal, documenting events between 1863 and 1869. Dr. Kelly and I do have several other artifacts that will be announced to the historical community after they are fully researched.

"Thank you all for being such a great audience. It has been a pleasure talking to you today, and as I mentioned, Dr. Kelly and I will be available for questions in the hotel lobby."

Dan stepped away from the podium, and Kate whispered to him, "I didn't know you were going to announce the existence of the gold coin."

"After this morning's break-in, I decided the safest thing to do was to put the coin in the public eye. I had the hotel manager move an exhibit case from the mezzanine level to the lobby to display the coin and the documents.

I also made a quick call to Brinks and arranged for guards and transportation of the documents and coin to the University.

"Let's go to the lobby. I imagine there will be a lot of questions."

CHAPTER SIX

Mugged in LA

Kate and Dan walked into the hotel lobby and immediately saw a crowd surrounding the display case. They could also see four armed guards at the corners of the exhibit case. Curious historians with questions for them.

After forty-five minutes, Veronica Bailey approached Dan and Kate and said, "That is a very impressive coin. If my memory is correct, there are only about a dozen of these currently known to exist. The coin is worth millions.

"It was an intelligent move, announcing the coin's existence to this group. You have effectively kept it out of the hands of a collector. Oh well, I am certain there are more of them hidden out there." Bailey then walked away toward the north entrance of the hotel on Hollywood Boulevard.

"Kate, we won round one of this prize fight, but unfortunately, we are destined to see more of her in the future."

An armored car arrived at the south entrance, and two guards entered the building with a silver-colored security case about the size of a brief case. Dan opened the exhibit case and carefully removed the two documents and placed them in an archival envelope. Then he put the 2.5-ounce fifty-dollar gold coin in a brown coin envelope, which was then placed in a small jewelry box.

The documents and the gold coin were then placed in the padded security case that was being transported to Stanford University. The guard handed him a receipt and took the case to the waiting armored car.

Dan and Kate took a seat in the hotel lobby and Dan said, "Now we have to find out more about Veronica Bailey."

"How are we going to get background information on her?" Kate asked.

Dan replied, "I am going to call Special Agent Jack Packard of the FBI. Do you remember him?"

"Wasn't he a graduate student with us at Stanford who dropped out and took a job as a policeman?"

"That's right, Kate. After two years with the Los Angeles Police Department, he was recruited to the FBI by J. Edgar Hoover. Hoover liked Packard's background and put him in charge of investigating jewelry and fine arts thefts."

Dan walked over to a phone booth in a hallway off the lobby and made a phone call to Packard then returned to where Kate was sitting. "What do you think about having a late lunch?" he asked her.

"Sure, where are we going?"

Dan smiled and said, "Pinks."

Kate rolled her eyes and said, "Okay, big spender."

They walked to the south entrance, and Kate handed the valet her claim tag. He hurried off and returned with her

Thunderbird a few minutes later. Dan gave the valet a tip as he opened the driver's side door for Kate. They drove off and Kate discussed Dan's affinity for junk food until they were in sight of Pink's hot dog stand. Kate parked on a street behind the stand, and they got in the queue in front of the hot dog stand.

"Dan, when will we meet with Packard?"

"Kate, that's why we are here. Packard loves this place, and I offered to buy him lunch. He should arrive in a few minutes."

It was three o'clock, and the line was surprisingly short; it took them only ten minutes to get to the head of the line. Kate ordered a chili dog, and Dan ordered a hot dog with mustard and onions and two hot dogs in one bun with chili, cheese, and mustard for Agent Packard. Kate and Dan found a table in a small patio area just as Jack Packard arrived.

"Perfect timing—and I can see you remember how I like my hot dog."

Dan shook Packard's hand and said, "Thanks for coming so quickly. We just had a run-in with someone that may be a black market collector, and I suspect you may have a file on her. Have you ever heard of a woman named Veronica Bailey?"

Jack put down his hot dog. "I don't have to go to my files to answer that. I have two active investigations looking into possible black market activity by Bailey. I can't give you the details but this beauty has excellent taste in art and fine coins."

Dan looked at Kate and said, "We think she attempted to steal a gold coin from us that is worth millions and will be following us to our next field research project here in California."

Dan went on, "If our project is a success, we may find Theodore Judah's lost gold, including two thousand fifty-dollar coins like the one Bailey tried to steal plus millions in gold dust and gold nuggets."

Packard said, "Knowing Veronica Bailey's background, I can safely say that she will try to steal the whole cache of gold at her first opportunity. Your situation is clearly related to my current investigation of Bailey, and if it is okay with you, I would like to monitor your next project."

"Thanks, Jack. Kate and I will send you a summary of our project plan and keep you posted on our schedule."

"Dan, I think we can do better than that," Jack replied. "How would you like to have a new assistant on your dig? The bureau would really like to catch your new friend in the act of stealing valuable artifacts."

Kate said, "With your background from Stanford, you would be perfect for our crew."

As they got up from the table, Packard asked for a complete list of the students in the crew so he could do background checks on all of them. "Of course, you realize Bailey will try to infiltrate your crew to get inside information."

Dan told him they would keep their eyes open and thanked him for his support. Dan and Kate walked back to the Thunderbird, and as they reached the car, Dan said, "We have one more stop before we return to the hotel."

"Where are we headed?"

"Let's go to Sixth and Hill Street to have your watch checked at a jewelry store."

"Darn, for a second, I thought you were going to buy me something."

Dan laughed. "Someday, sweetheart."

When they reached Sixth and Hill, they parked near Pershing Square and entered an upscale jewelry store. A well-dressed man walked out of the back room and said, "Dan, it is great to see you again! You always bring me such interesting items to work on. What do you have for me today?"

Dan introduced Kate to him and said, "Kate has a pocket watch I would like you to look at, David."

Kate opened her handbag and pulled out her gold pocket watch and chain. David took the watch and said, "This is a beautiful timepiece. Come with me into the workshop, and I'll take a look."

As he opened the watch, he told Kate it had incredible craftsmanship and was most likely made no later than 1870. The watch mechanism was made by the American Watch Company, and the jeweler's mark was stamped "Bailey Sacramento." This told the jeweler that the watchmaker was James Bailey of Sacramento. The stamped number "725" signified that the case was made of eighteen-carat gold. "The workmanship is excellent, and it appears to be in perfect working condition," he told her. "The engraving on the outside of the case was hand engraved by a skilled craftsman. The engraving inside the watch was also hand engraved, but not by the same person who engraved the outside of the watch. This watch was made to railroad standards and is probably extremely accurate."

"There is engraving on the inside of the watch?" Dan asked.

David replied, "Yes, it says: *ECV Stake is Found where The Sacramento Crossed CPRR.*"

"Kate, Smiley was definitely referring to the miners' investment in Judah's plan to purchase back the Central Pacific

Railroad. This inscription validates Doc Strong's journal entries and hopefully will help lead us to the gold's hiding place."

The jeweler told Kate she had an extremely valuable timepiece and thanked her for allowing him to look at it. "If you have a few minutes, I would like to clean and lubricate the watch movement."

Kate smiled and said, "That is very kind of you. I would love to have it cleaned up."

Dan told David they would take a short walk and return before he closed the shop. Dan then took the journal and a leather bag out of his briefcase and asked if he could leave them in the safe while they were out.

"Certainly," said the jeweler.

By this time, Kate was fixated on the jewelry case containing diamond engagement rings. She pointed at a white gold ring with a large brilliant-cut diamond surrounded by two diamond baguettes and said, "That is my dream ring!"

Dan instantly said, "It's time to go, Kate."

They left the store and were walking in the direction of Pershing Square when they heard a car drive up and stop behind them. Dan turned his head and saw a man in a dark suit behind them, pointing a revolver at him. The man told them to place the briefcase and handbag on the ground in front of him. Dan placed the briefcase on the ground, but Kate refused to give up the purse.

The man grabbed the purse, and Kate instantly swung it into the gun, knocking it to the sidewalk. She then spun around and, before he could react, landed a reverse roundhouse kick to his groin, followed by a leg sweep to the back of his knees. The man dropped to the ground in pain. Before Dan could reach the gun on the sidewalk, another man inside the car pointed a gun at them and told them to turn around and drop to their knees. Kate and Dan followed his directions and heard the two men pick up the briefcase and handbag. Just as they expected to be shot, they heard the car doors slam and saw a dark blue sedan screech by them. Dan scrambled for the gun that was still on the sidewalk, but the car was too far away to get a clear shot at it.

"Are you okay, Kate? That was crazy—he could have shot you!"

"I am really ticked off!" Kate exclaimed. "That was my favorite purse. But at least they didn't get any of the artifacts."

Dan said, "That's strike two for Bailey. I have a hunch she will try again soon. I wonder if she will want to hurt us in the process to teach us a lesson."

Kate and Dan returned to the jewelry store and told David about the attack, and then Dan used the phone to contact Packard. The jeweler brought Kate's pocket watch out of the back room. In addition to servicing the watch, he had also carefully polished the watchcase, and it glistened under the jewelry store lighting.

"How much do I owe you?" she asked.

He smiled. "It's my pleasure, especially considering the amount restoration work Dan has brought me from the university's collections."

Dan told him, "In light of the robbery attempt, I think it might be a good idea to have the watch sent to the university by courier."

Kate nodded in approval and handed the watch back to David. "Thank you for working on my watch."

The jeweler replied, "I will take good care of it and make certain it reaches you at the university, young lady." Kate gave him a quick kiss on his cheek and said, "You're the best."

Dan then walked into the back room with David and retrieved the journal and leather bag from the safe. David also handed Dan a small box, which Dan placed in his pocket before returning to the showroom.

They walked out the front door of the shop, and Dan said, "I think we've had enough excitement for one day. I owe you a nice dinner. Let's head back to the hotel, and after we freshen up, I want to have dinner with you at the Brown Derby."

That evening, back the hotel, Dan knocked on Kate's door. When she opened the door, he could see she was dressed in a dazzling, azure blue cocktail dress that complemented her blue eyes and rich pink skin tones. "Wow!" he said. "Every eye in the Derby is going to be on you when you walk into the restaurant."

Dan took Kate's arm as they entered the lobby and had the doorman hail a cab for them. Dan opened the door for Kate and told the driver to take them to the Brown Derby. When they entered the restaurant, they could see the waiters were very busy serving well-dressed diners. Kate and Dan were seated in a booth beside a wall of framed sketches of Hollywood's elite movie stars. When they looked around the dining room, they could see several people looking in their direction.

Dan said, "They are trying to figure out who this beautiful starlet is."

Kate blushed. The waiter handed her a menu. "Dan, did you see Cary Grant in the corner booth?" she asked.

"Yes, I saw him, and I see Jack Lemmon in the booth behind you."

She slowly turned her head to sneak a peek. Lemmon smiled when he saw her turn her head and gave her a wink. Dan chuckled and said, "I bet that made your day."

After eating dinner, Dan pulled a small box out of his jacket pocket and gave it to Kate. She opened the jewelry box and saw the diamond ring she had admired at the jewelry store. He said, "I would like to ask you something very important tonight. We have always been constant companions since we were kids and partners as students and research archeologists. During all that time, we have been much more than friends. I love you, Kate, and I would love to take the next step in our relationship."

"Will you marry me, Kate?"

"Dan, of course I will. I have dreamed of marrying you since high school."

He stood up, went to her side of the booth, and put the ring on her finger, and they kissed. As he got up to return to his seat, he saw Jack Lemmon standing at their booth. "I could not help but overhear your proposal. I would like to congratulate you and your beautiful fiancée, and wish you love and good fortune in your life together."

Lemmon then gave Kate a kiss on her cheek and shook Dan's hand. Dan said, "Thank you, Mr. Lemmon."

"This was definitely my pleasure—I love kissing a beautiful woman." Lemmon then returned to his booth.

Dan and Kate finished the Brown Derby's famous grapefruit cake and walked out to Vine Street. Kate said, "It is such a beautiful night. I would like to walk back to the hotel."

Dan told her he would like that. They walked a half block and turned left onto Hollywood Blvd. "Kate, aren't you afraid we might run into more of Bailey's men?" he asked.

Kate wrapped her arm around Dan and said, "You will take care of me." Several blocks later, they approached a small group of people leaving the Paramount and Grauman's Chinese Theaters. Kate said, "I can never get enough of the sights, sounds, and history of Hollywood."

Dan said, "It definitely has its advantages over working in the desert sands of Egypt."

They entered the Roosevelt lobby and went up to their rooms, where they could hear the sounds of a party at the Tropicana Bar below them. Dan walked straight to Kate's room, and when she opened her door, she held his hand, pulled him inside, and closed the door behind him.

HOLLYWOOD SIGN
Photo by Massimo Catarinella

CHAPTER SEVEN

Hooray for Hollywood

Early the next morning, Dan and Kate went to a hotel conference room in the lower level of the hotel, where a meeting with their graduate students had been scheduled. They could see twenty familiar faces of students who had previously worked with them on their Egypt and Capri research projects. The students were busily eating a working breakfast of pastries, orange juice, milk, and coffee.

Jack Packard entered the room and grabbed a donut before walking up to Dan and Kate. Dan said, "Jack, aren't you afraid you will blow your cover, eating a donut?"

Packard smiled and sat down at the table near them. Dan started the meeting a few minutes later. "Welcome to Hollywood. Dr. Kelly and I both thank you for joining our new research project. You have worked with us before and contributed to greatly to our very successful digs, both at the Villa

Jovis in Capri and in Egypt. Our next project brings us home to California for a very different historical investigation: documenting the events and places involved with the building of the Central Pacific Railroad."

"We have one new member of our team for this project. His name is Jack Packard. Dr. Packard was a classmate of Dr. Kelly and me at Stanford, and we thought his skills would be a great addition to this project."

All of you attended the historical society meeting at the conference this week, so you are aware of the documents and the gold coin that was made public. There are several other documents and artifacts that I have not announced yet that we also will be working with during this dig. During this project, we will be researching and documenting important sites and validating events that have been lost to the historical record.

"A major goal is to use your archeology skills to study historic sites in the mother lode area and on the Central Pacific Railroad route, crossing the Sierra. Unlike the monumental structures we researched in Italy, many of the sites have been reduced to their original stone foundations, which are disappearing as each year passes."

Dan then placed a Xerox copy of Doc Strong's journal on the table and told the audience, "This journal will be our guide. Yesterday you heard about Judah's gold and the Clamper gold hoard. These treasures are part of the folk tales of California's history. They are both specifically mentioned in Doc Strong's journal, and confirming their existence is a major goal of this project." Dan reminded them, "We are not treasure hunters, and if we are fortunate enough to find the gold and validate its existence, it will become a vital part of California's history and will be placed on public display in an appropriate museum setting.

"I have to warn you, during this dig you may be contacted by treasure hunters who are active in the hills. Be careful to protect your work so that a treasure hunter will not try to disrupt your site and remove artifacts. Contact Kate or me if you see anything out of the ordinary."

Kate then gave each member of the team their specific work assignments and divided them into two groups. She took her team to the back of the room, while Dan assembled his team in the front of the room. They worked until lunchtime, when Dan called both teams together and said, "You have all received your assignments, and we look forward to seeing you in Murphys in a few days."

Packard walked up to Kate and Dan after the conference room had cleared and told them he just received the ballistics report from the gun that had been dropped on the sidewalk when they were robbed. "The pattern on the test bullet shot from that gun is a match for a slug that wounded a guard during a museum theft. The theft is one of the cases I am already working on, and Veronica Bailey is the prime suspect.

"Make sure you keep all your artifacts secure in a safe place."

Dan opened an old lawyer-style briefcase and showed him Doc Strong's journal and a leather bag that contained the other artifacts. "These will not leave my sight."

Packard said, " Be careful. I will see you in Murphys in a few days."

Dan and Kate walked up to the hotel lobby, and as they walked, Dan asked Kate, "Do you want to follow up on Marilyn's invitation and watch them shooting her film at Metro Studio?"

"Sure, that sounds like it might be interesting."

They walked to the hotel's south entrance, and the valet brought Kate's car. As they left the hotel, Dan said, "Let's get a quick lunch at Scrivner's Drive-In and then drive to MGM." Kate drove a few blocks to Sunset and Cahuenga and pulled her Thunderbird into the crowded parking area of the hamburger stand. They ordered their cheeseburgers and Cokes, and Dan noticed a dark blue sedan park at the curb outside the parking lot.

"Kate, I think we have company again. See the car that just pulled up to the curb? It looks like the same car from the jewelry store."

They finished their lunch, and Dan switched over to the driver's side of the car. He drove to the exit from the drive-in that was farthest away from the blue sedan and sped into the busy traffic on Sunset Boulevard. The blue sedan was facing the wrong direction to give chase. It had to pull into Scrivner's parking lot to get to Sunset Boulevard. The blue car had some trouble driving through the parking spaces, narrowly missing people as it sped by. By the time it reached Sunset Boulevard, the red Thunderbird was already three blocks away.

Dan made a left turn a few blocks later, then made a right turn a block after that. He kept making turns while moving in the direction of MGM's Culver City Studio seven miles away.

"Kate, I am certain that car was trying to follow us. He can't know our destination, so the safest thing to do is get into the studio, where there is security watching the gate. MGM has a large police force to keep unwanted people out of the lot. We can call Packard and then watch them film Marilyn's movie in one of the sound stages."

They reached the gate of MGM studio a few minutes later, and Dan handed the gate guard Marilyn's card. The guard gave them directions to the sound stage and told them where to park. Dan told the guard about the car following them and gave him Packard's FBI office number. Dan asked the guard to call Packard to coordinate an escort back to their hotel. The guard then waved them into the studio lot.

As they drove to the parking area, they could see a large group of actors in costume for the movie production of *Porgy and Bess* that was also filming that day. They parked the car and walked directly to the sound stage for Marilyn's movie production. They walked up to the door of the stage and could see a small sign that said *Not Tonight, Josephine!* Before they entered the stage, two unusual-looking women walked out the door dressed in flapper outfits from the Roaring Twenties.

One of the women looked at Kate and said in a baritone voice, "Hello, sweetie! I remember you from the Derby last night, wearing that knockout blue dress."

Kate and Dan were speechless for a moment. Then the woman laughed and said, "Excuse me, I guess you don't recognize me in this dress and makeup. I'm Jack Lemmon, and Tony and I are all dolled up for a film they are shooting today."

Dan and Kate suddenly realized that they were looking at Jack Lemmon and Tony Curtis in drag. Kate asked, "Are you filming with Marilyn Monroe in *Not Tonight, Josephine!*?"

Lemmon responded, "Yes, whenever she decides to show up. *Not Tonight, Josephine!* is the working name of the movie. It will be called *Some Like It Hot* when it is released next year."

Tony Curtis asked, "Jack, who is this beauty?"

"Control yourself, Tony. She just got engaged to this gentleman last night at the Derby, and they look like a great match."

Lemmon told them that Marilyn was in the makeup department and, with a little bit of luck, would be on he set in a few minutes. "She is a little upset that they will be filming in black and white instead of Technicolor," he said. "The producer discovered that the heavy makeup Tony and I have to wear looks green on color film."

He told them he and Curtis were headed to the Commissary to have a little fun, and they wobbled off down the street in high heels, talking to surprised actors on the street in high falsetto voices.

Dan said, "What a character. He sure enjoys getting into his role."

Dan and Kate showed Marilyn's card to the guard at the door of the sound stage, walked to the visitor's area behind the cameras, and took a seat. They had waited only a few minutes before Marilyn arrived. She gave them a wave as she walked onto the set and began going over the script with the director. The crew had to shoot several takes of the same scene; Marilyn appeared to be having problems getting her lines correct and seemed a bit confused.

Dan and Kate stayed in the sound stage for about an hour; then they decided to see if Packard and his men had arrived. They walked out of the soundstage toward Kate's car and could see two men in suits standing beside it.

"Dan, those are the two gunmen from last night!"

Dan Kate quickly changed direction and headed back toward the soundstage. They could see the two men running in their direction. The guard was not at the stage door, so they kept running until they joined a large group of black actors milling around in the street outside another soundstage.

They ducked into the stage and could see the production was in between shots. They could not see a guard, so they ran out a doorway at the side of the sound stage into an outdoor set. A gunshot sounded as they ran through this set with the two men in pursuit. Surprisingly, none of the actors and production crew reacted to the gunshots. They seemed to think it was a studio prank.

The gunmen were in close pursuit when Dan and Kate ran onto a street between several soundstages. Dan and Kate could see the Studio Commissary straight ahead of them. They raced through a small group of actors and ran into the Commissary, where they found two studio policemen eating at a small table.

Dan quickly explained their situation and gave them Packard's number. One of the policemen went to a phone and called the security office, gave them Dan's description of the gunmen, and told them to seal the gates of the studio until they were found. Then the policeman called Packard and found out he was at the gate of the studio, waiting for Dan and Kate. The two policemen escorted them to Kate's car and followed as they drove to the front gate.

The gate guard then told the police officer, "I have bad news; two men in dark suits left the studio just before the FBI arrived and disappeared down the street."

Packard walked up to Dan and Kate and said, "What am I going to do with you two? You attract trouble wherever you go."

"No, Jack, trouble is finding us wherever we go. Bailey is one determined bitch who won't quit until she gets what she wants."

Packard told them that he would follow them back to the hotel and arrange to have an FBI agent inside the hotel to watch them. He also told them he would not be able to have agents watch them on the road until he got approval from FBI management.

Kate and Dan drove back to the Roosevelt and went to the poolside bar for a drink and snack. Dan ordered his customary rum and Coke, and Kate ordered a shot of Irish whiskey.

They talked about the gunmen and concluded that Bailey would continue the attacks until they agreed to give her a share of the gold coins. They also felt Bailey would try to get all the documents and artifacts so she could find the gold by herself and keep the entire treasure for her collection. "We would just be a nuisance to her at that point, and she would try to eliminate us," Dan said. "We can't let Veronica Bailey run our lives; we have worked too hard to have this project slip through our hands. We need to be careful and not change our plans. Packard cannot protect us without putting us in a safe house. The only way to end this harassment is to have the FBI catch her and her men in the act."

CHAPTER EIGHT

Hollywood Hills Adventure

"**K**ate, how would you like to take a romantic drive to see the lights of Los Angeles from the Griffith Park Observatory?"

"Is that safe, Dan?"

Dan said that he would tell Packard where they were headed, so he could have his men watch the area. "There are only a few roads in and out of the observatory, and they would be able to catch anyone following us," he explained.

Dan went to a phone at the bar and called Packard to explain his plan to him. Packard liked the idea and told him he and a team of agents would cover the roads entering the Griffith Park Observatory, starting at seven o'clock. He chuckled as he said, "They should have no trouble spotting Kate's bright red Thunderbird."

Dan returned to Kate and told her what had been arranged. They lingered by the pool until about six-thirty and then picked up Kate's car at the hotel's back entrance. Dan took the wheel. "Packard told me to drive up Vermont Avenue to the observatory and return on Western," he told Kate.

They drove a short distance on Hollywood Boulevard to Vermont Avenue, and after a few residential blocks, they started up the mountain and drove past the Greek Theater. A short distance later, the road curved to the left onto the access road for the observatory. Dan parked the car in a curved parking area in front of the observatory.

Kate and Dan walked through a park-like area past the Astronomer's Monument in front of the observatory's north door. They strolled around the building to the south, where they found a bench in an open viewing area with a fantastic view of the Los Angeles skyline. They looked down and to the right and could also see the lights of Hollywood, twinkling a thousand feet below them. The Hollywood sign was glowing near the top of a mountain peak to their far right.

They had been enjoying the view for about thirty minutes when a man came out of the shadows with a gun pointed them. The gunman said, "Come with me, my boss has some questions for you two."

They both dropped to the ground behind the bench, as Dan said, "Where the hell are Packard's men? We are bottled up here with no escape route!"

They heard the sound of a bullet hitting the concrete bench, then the sound of sirens approaching. Several police cars and FBI cars drove up into the observation area, and the lone gunman jumped off the observation deck down to a small trail that ran through a wooded area below the observatory. Packard ran up to Dan and Kate and asked, "Are you two alright?"

"Yes, Jack, the gunman managed to miss us again, but Kate and I are starting to feel like targets in a shooting gallery."

Packard explained, "The gunman must have hiked in on that trail after he followed you here. There were three cars that drove past the observatory, but they did not look like they were following you. My men will search the woods below and try to catch them, but there are a lot of places they could hide their car." He told them he would follow them downhill to Hollywood and gave directions how to get there on Western. Kate and Dan returned to the car and drove off. Dan missed the left turn onto Western and turned left when the road ended at Mt. Hollywood Road.

Dan and Kate could not see Packard's car following behind them. "Kate, I missed the turn, and we are driving on the wrong road. We must have lost Packard."

They continued on Mt. Hollywood Road around a short hairpin curve to the left. Dan could see a familiar blue sedan following close behind. He could tell it was not Packard's car or any of the police cars that were at the observatory. "Kate, we have problem. Bailey's men are tailing us again, and I am not too familiar with the roads up here."

Dan stomped on the accelerator as he rounded a large hairpin turn to the right and put a little distance between the two cars. He took a slight left turn onto the Mulholland Highway and picked up his speed, zigzagging down the road until he took a sharp right turn onto Mt. Lee Road. He sped around a large hairpin turn to the right, then one to the left, and he could see downhill that the blue sedan was still following them.

"I have a really bad feeling that this road may reach a dead end."

Dan saw a large radio tower above them and said. "Shit, I know where we are. That tower is right above the big Hollywood sign, and the road dead-ends there."

"I have a plan. Kate, in a minute, we are going to round a very sharp turn to the left, and I am going to stop and let you out. Take the trail below the road to the Hollywood sign and hide in front of the big 'W'."

Dan screeched around the curve and made a sudden stop. Kate disappeared down the side of the hill. Dan then sped to the gate of the tower area and made a fast U-turn, stopping at the extreme right side of the roadway with the view of the Thunderbird blocked by the mountainside above him. He revved up the engine and accelerated with smoke coming from the tires straight at the approaching blue sedan. The driver of the sedan panicked and made a sharp right turn, launching his car off the side of the road down the hill, narrowly missing the "H" in the Hollywood sign. The car continued to roll down the hill and came to rest on the mountainside.

Dan ran back to the edge of the road and could see Kate climbing the path up to the road. She yelled to Dan, "Next time, tell me to hide behind the "D!" That scared the bejeebies out of me, Dan!"

"Sorry, Kate, but that was the only way I could keep you safe."

Dan told Kate that he had read about a driver that drove off this road about ten years ago and took out the "H." "I figured the 'W' was far enough away from where the car would go, and I did not want you to go too far and slide down the mountainside in the dark."

"Okay, Dan, that's enough excitement for one night. Let's get back to the hotel and lock ourselves in our rooms."

They drove straight back to the Roosevelt. Packard approached them in the lobby and said, "Please tell me you didn't have anything to do with the car that almost wiped out the Hollywood sign tonight?"

Packard told them everyone in Hollywood could see the fire that the wreck started. Dan said, "Yes, we were there and managed to get rid of Bailey's hired guns that have been using us for target practice."

Packard informed them that there was an FBI agent in the hotel as well as hotel security that would be watching out for them that night. He also told them they would not have an escort driving home to Sacramento, but he had contacted a commander at the California Highway Patrol about their situation and sent an alert to all highway patrol offices in the Central and San Joaquin Valley to keep an eye out for them.

"So, drive carefully," he said.

Dan and Kate then went straight to their room and double locked the door.

CHAPTER NINE

Highway 99

The next morning, Dan and Kate brought their luggage to the south entrance of the hotel, where a valet had Kate's Thunderbird waiting. After loading up their luggage Dan asked Kate if it was okay if he drove. "Sure, I was not looking forward to the drive over the Grapevine, the steep mountain downgrade and curves makes me nervous."

They drove around to Hollywood Boulevard, and as they passed Grauman's, they heard a band playing "Hooray For Hollywood." Kate said, "Maybe a famous celebrity is getting footprints made."

An hour later they were on Highway 99, passing over Tejon Summit and starting the steep downhill drive into California's Central Valley. Dan said, "This section of highway can be extremely dangerous if you encounter a runaway big rig. Can you smell the smoke from the trucks' overheated brakes?"

Suddenly, Dan noticed a truck and trailer closing on them in the rearview mirror. The truck was driving too fast for the grade, and the truck was almost on their back bumper.

"Hold on, Kate, this guy is trying to run us off the road!"

Fortunately, the T-Bird was quick and maneuverable. After a couple of close calls, Dan stomped on the accelerator and managed to put some distance between them. They then started down the steepest part of the highway grade, and Dan could see dark smoke spewing out of the truck's two exhaust stacks.

This idiot is accelerating that truck down the grade. I will maneuver behind him the next time he makes a run at us."

Dan swung the car to the far right of the lane and stomped on the brakes, and the truck and trailer went flying past them. Dan could see a puff of gray smoke start coming from the truck's brakes. Dan could see the red light of a Highway Patrol cruiser in his rearview mirror, the cruiser passed their car, and got behind the truck and as it pulled off to the side of the highway.

Dan stopped on the side of the road a safe distance from the truck. The officer approached the car from the rear and asked, "Are you two alright? I saw that diesel rig try to run you off the road." When he saw that they were unharmed, he went on, "Are you Daniel Strong and Katherine Kelly? We were warned to keep an eye out for you." After checking their identification, he told them the truck driver would be arrested for dangerous driving.

"Drive carefully," the officer said, and returned to his car.

An hour later they reached Bakersfield. As they drove into town, they could see a huge arched sign across the entire highway that said "BAKERSFIELD." When they got closer, they could see the sign was actually a walkway, connecting two sections of a hotel on both sides of the highway.

Dan pulled into a Standard Service station adjoining the Bakersfield Inn to get gas, and an army of gas station attendants came over to the car.

Dan said, "Fill'r up."

The attendants cleaned the windshield and checked the oil, water and transmission fluid levels. They checked the air pressure on the tires, and one of the attendants came to Dan and said, "Wow, you are lucky you turned in for gas. All four of your tires have slashes, and they need to be replaced."

Dan asked if they could replace the tires, and the attendant said, "No problem, sir; it should only take a few minutes, but I have to check if we have the tires in stock."

He returned a couple minutes later and told him that they only had two of the correct tires in stock, but he had checked with their supplier, and they could get two more tires within a couple of hours.

"Dan said, "That sounds great, but there is no rush; we will stay at the Bakersfield Inn tonight and pick up the car in the morning. Go ahead and replace the tires, change the oil, and give her a tune-up."

Dan picked up Kate's and his bags, and they walked toward the entrance of the Spanish-style hotel. Dan told Kate that this was a great place to spend the night; the Bakersfield Inn was an oasis in the searing heat of California's Central Valley.

Dan explained, "The highway brings a high level of traffic through here, and it is a popular resort stop. Believe it or not, there are a number of popular nightclubs near here that have featured Hollywood celebrities who stay here at the Bakersfield Inn."

Kate and Dan walked into the spacious lobby and arranged for a room near the pool courtyard. They walked through a palm-surrounded courtyard with beautifully landscaped tropical gardens and reached an arched beige, stucco-covered walkway near a large swimming pool. Their room was just a few steps away.

Kate and Dan put their bags in the room, and Kate said, "That pool looks very inviting; let's take a swim."

"That works for me."

They changed into their swimsuits, and each grabbed a towel and headed straight to the pool. Kate put her towel and a dark brown bottle of sun lotion on a lounge chair and dove into the pool. Dan followed, and they swam laps for few minutes before relaxing in the afternoon sun. Kate climbed the ladder out of the pool and dried off before reclining in a lounge chair. "Dan, could you help me put on some sun lotion?"

Dan climbed out of the pool, took the dark brown glass bottle, and poured some of the clear liquid into his hand and massaged it into to Kate's fair skin.

"Ahh. That feels feel great, Dan."

"Kate, don't stay in the sun too long; you will get as red as a lobster in this valley sun."

Dan jumped back into the pool and swam for a few more minutes, then went back to Kate. "Time is up. I don't want you sunburned."

They walked back to the room, showered, and changed into their dinner clothes. They then walked through the courtyard to a tall, beige building with curved Mexican tiles on the roof. They entered the restaurant and were seated at a table in the center of the dining room and given the restaurant menu.

Dan ordered a shrimp cocktail and a New York sirloin steak, while Kate ordered an Italian salad and what was described as a broiled "San Kenteen" lobster.

As they walked through the lobby after dinner, a tall, well-dressed man approached them and said, "Dan and Kate, imagine running into you here way out in the middle of nowhere! Would you care to join me in the lounge for an after dinner drink?"

Dan immediately said, "Cut the crap, Damian, this is not a coincidence. What are you up to this time?"

The man was not shaken by Dan's comment and said, "Kate, you look stunning as usual. It is wonderful to see my favorite archeology team again.

"Dan, you are correct. I have intentionally come here to meet with you two. Veronica Bailey has employed me to conduct a study here in California." Dan responded, "Does your study involve the history of the Central Pacific Railroad, by any chance?"

Damian responded, "Yes, it does, and it also involves work in the Mother Lode area of California as well."

"Stay clear of us, Damian! I will not allow a repeat of your activities at our digs in Capri and Egypt."

"Daniel, I am sorry you feel that way. I am really looking forward to seeing you two at the Murphys project site. I have some very important information concerning where Judah's gold coins were hidden in the Sierra.

"I really wish you would accept Veronica Bailey's offer of partnership. I like you two a great deal, and Ms. Bailey's tactics are extremely dangerous, as you have already discovered."

Damian starting walking in the direction of the cocktail lounge and said, "Have a safe trip."

Kate looked at Dan and said, "Just what we need, both Bradford Damian and Veronica Bailey sabotaging our research project."

Dan and Kate were surprised that Damian had information on Judah's gold and speculated that the information came from the Pinkerton report that went to James Bailey in 1866.

Dan wondered how Damian knew their first dig site would be at Murphys. Kate guessed that it would have been easy for Bailey to find out the destination of the students' bus.

They returned to their room, and before turning in, they talked about their plans for the drive to Sacramento in the morning. Dan and Kate got an early start in the morning. After a quick breakfast, they walked back to the Standard Service station. They checked with one of the attendants, and he drove the Thunderbird out of the garage area of the station. They noticed that attendants had not only done the work Dan asked for but also had washed and hand-waxed the car's exterior as well.

"Wow, Dan, my T-Bird looks as good as it did on the showroom floor." Dan paid the bill and made certain that all of the gas station crew received a generous tip.

They drove out of the gas station on to Highway 99 and started driving north toward Sacramento. During the trip Dan noticed several different Highway Patrol cars following them at a distance.

They made two stops during their trip. Kate saw a Giant Orange mid-morning and wanted a fresh-squeezed orange juice, and in the afternoon they stopped in Lodi at an A&W stand for burgers and a mug of root beer before getting gas at a nearby gas station.

They reached Sacramento in the afternoon and drove straight to Dan's mansion in Sacramento's "Fabulous Forties" neighborhood. He grabbed his bag and briefcase and said, "I will pick you up in the morning about eight o'clock, Kate."

Kate then drove around the block to her family's Tudor-style mansion, which shared a gated backyard fence with Dan's home.

MURPHYS HOTEL

Photo by Ralph Orlandella (Author)

CHAPTER TEN

Mother Lode Travels

Dan arrived in front of Kate's house at eight o'clock sharp the next morning in his 1955 black and silver Buick Roadmaster. He walked up to her front door, and Kate greeted him with a kiss.

"Dan, you can't imagine how excited my mom and dad were when they noticed my ring. We better get out of town quickly, or they will keep us here all day."

"I am all packed and ready to go," said Kate.

Dan placed all her luggage and several boxes of project files in the trunk of the Buick. Kate placed a couple small boxes in the backseat of the car and said, "Let's go! I always love the excitement of the first day of a dig."

They sped off down the tree-lined street and headed straight up the foothills of the Sierra. They passed through Sutter Creek and took Highway 49 through Jackson and San Andreas. They reached Angels Camp at about ten o'clock.

Dan pulled into a small parking lot in front of a Gold Rush museum that had once been a hardware store. The museum was filled with a large collection of mining equipment that had been a vital part of the Gold Rush era. There was everything from a Studebaker wheelbarrow to a twenty-foot-long water nozzle, once used for hydraulic mining that could wash away an entire mountainside.

They walked inside, and the owner of the private museum recognized Dan and welcomed them. "It's nice to see you again, Dan."

Dan looked around the museum and said, "Richard, you have a terrific collection of mining equipment. I'm very pleased that the museum is preserving all of this, so future generations can get a glimpse of the magnitude of mining operations that took place in this area."

Richard said, "I think I may have something you will be interested in. I heard that your new research project concerns the building of the Central Pacific Railroad, and these items have a link to the railroad and the Big Four."

Richard went behind his desk and returned with a box. Dan and Kate could see it contained a leather-bound notebook, a large Colt 1861 Navy revolver, and a gun case full of accessories. He explained that a longtime resident of Angels Camp brought this in to the museum. "She told me the notebook belonged to a Pinkerton detective named John Richardson," he said. "The notebook entries explain how he was hired by the Central Pacific Railroad to find some sort of document and a fortune in gold that had been taken from the Big Four. Richardson did not catch them, but stayed here in the Mother Lode area for the next twenty years, searching for a hidden Clamper treasure of gold."

Richard warned Dan that the powder flask had been sealed, and there definitely was black powder in it. He thought it extremely unlikely that the powder would burn, but the seal was intact.

Dan asked to pay for the contents of the box, but the museum owner refused. "The lady that donated this wants it to go to museum."

Dan took out his checkbook. "If I can't pay for it, I insist on making a donation to your museum."

Dan and Kate walked out to the car and started the short drive to Murphys.

Kate examined the journal from the box for a few minutes. "Dan, Detective Richardson's notes match Doc Strong's journal entries," she said. She went on to explain that although Doc Strong was careful not to mention Judah's gold or the miners' gold, Richardson's notes specifically mentioned both. Doc Strong's entries were obviously intended to keep the cargo vague, in case the wrong person got his journal. "Richardson's notes specifically mention Judah's gold and the locations that it could be hidden," Kate explained. "His notes are extremely detailed and must have been used when he wrote his formal Pinkerton report for Bailey and the Big Four."

"It's fantastic that Doc Strong and Richardson's notes match," Dan replied. "They should get us close to the hiding place, but I still believe your watch has the critical clue to the exact location of Judah's gold. Judah's surveyor's plumb bob and the spike will be needed to physically open the gold's hiding place."

Dan turned onto Murphy's Main Street. They could see one team of students at work in a vacant lot next to the Compere

store building and the second team down the street working
outside the Jones Apothecary building. They turned off Main
Street when they reached the Murphys Hotel, drove past the
old Murphys jailhouse, and continued a short distance to
Murphys Park. Kate looked across the street from the park and
said, "Unbelievable, the camp is set up exactly like our campsite on Capri."

The camp was arranged on an open field near a stream
with a row of ten four-person tents and two large meeting tents.
The camp also had a small Airstream trailer equipped with a
photographic darkroom.

They parked next to the last four-person tent. Dan and
Kate each had their own tent outfitted with a bunk, desk, and
worktable. Dan and Kate went to the large headquarters tent
after they had loaded their gear into their own tents.

There was a great deal of activity in the camp. In addition
to the student archeologists, there was a crew of workers hired
to assist the project by cooking and doing work like operating
heavy equipment at the dig site.

There was a large bulletin board outside the headquarters
tent. Dan and Kate could see a note posted on the board that
said there would be a team meeting at 1:00 p.m. at the picnic
tables in the park.

"Kate, let's take a quick tour of the Main Street digs before
lunch."

They walked back to Main Street and met with the two
teams, working at opposite ends of the street. One team was
busy measuring and photographing the Murphys Hotel and
the Jones Apothecary building across the street. The second
team was at the end of the street, plotting the foundation of

a building in a vacant lot. Both teams shared the same sense of excitement that Kate and Dan always felt when they started work on a new site.

The students had already located and identified several building sites that had been reduced to a few foundation stones. An excited student ran up to Kate and Dan and told them she had found the foundation of the long lost miners' "Hall of Comparative Ovations," located right next to the Compere store building.

Dan and Kate stopped at a few of the Main Street shops and talked to the business owners. They were extremely happy to have the project in town. They all felt the discoveries would document the importance of their community during the Gold Rush and result in more tourism. Dan and Kate then walked back to the camp, filled their plates at the kitchen, and sat down at one of the park's picnic tables. Jack Packard arrived and sat down beside them at the table. "I hear you had a wild ride drive home from Hollywood," he said.

Packard told them that the Highway Patrol had kept an eye on them after the truck incident. "They did not have any trouble locating Kate's bright red Thunderbird as you drove through valley," he said. "The two gunmen that had the downhill ride at the Hollywood sign survived and are in custody at the City of Angels Hospital. We checked them out, and they are both hired hit men who usually do work for the Mafia.

"Yesterday, the truck driver sang like a bird when our agent questioned him. He told them that a dark-haired lady approached him in a coffee shop in Gorman and gave him an envelope full of hundred-dollar bills, to scare you driving down the hill."

Packard then informed Dan and Kate that two of the project workers assisting the students were undercover FBI agents, and he had arranged for an alarm system for the Murphys jailhouse so that it could be used for storing any important artifacts that may be found.

Dan told Packard that Veronica Bailey had hired Bradford Damian, a black-market treasure hunter, to find Judah's gold. He explained that they had run into Damian in the past. "He is a very talented archeologist who found it more lucrative to become a black-market antiquities dealer."

Packard said, "I have a file on Mr. Damian. He may be involved in a recent museum theft I am investigating."

At 1:00 p.m., all the students gathered at the picnic tables for their meeting. Kate and Dan stood in the middle of the table area and thanked them for the excellent job they had done, setting up the campsite. Kate told the students that they were pleased to have such an experienced team of archeologists to work with. She explained they would be researching a series of separate dig locations during this project. "The merchants here in Murphys are excited to have you working in their town and have said they will give you any support you need when you are researching their historic buildings," she said. "You have been divided into two teams and have all been given your work assignments."

Dan then spoke to the group and outlined the entire series of digs they would be working on during the project. "As you heard at the Hollywood conference, the project is based on the writings in Doc Strong's journal and travels through the Sierra mountain range. You also heard that Doc Strong was entrusted with Theodore Judah's payment of gold coins from the Big Four, and he initially hid the gold coins along with gold from the treasury of the miner's E Clampus Vitus treasury.

"The Clamper gold was their investment stake in buying out the Big Four's ownership in the Central Pacific Railroad. Doc Strong's journal never specifically mentions this gold. It does give a narrative of his travels, however. He did this to safeguard the location of the gold, in case his journal fell into the hands of the wrong people. The journal is missing one page, which may contain the details of the gold's hiding place. Dr. Kelly and I have artifacts that give clues to the exact location of the hiding place, and if you are fortunate, your work at each site will fill in the missing puzzle pieces and lead us to the hiding place of Judah's gold.

"Doc Strong and miner Jim Smiley promised Judah they would protect the money he had raised to purchase back the Central Pacific Railroad. When Judah died, the Associates were afraid that his partners would use the option-to-purchase document to buy out their shares in the railroad for four hundred thousand dollars. Charles Crocker convinced Central Pacific Railroad board member James Bailey to hire Pinkerton detectives to find and return the option-to-purchase document and, if possible, retrieve the gold as well.

"Dr. Kelly and I believe Doc Strong and Jim Smiley initially hid the gold here in Murphys in 1863. In 1866, Central Pacific Railroad's first assistant chief engineer Lewis Clement, a close friend and student of Judah, warned Doc Strong what was going on."

"The journal tells us that Doc Strong went to Murphys and warned Jim Smiley and the miners that the detectives were on their way. There is a chance that the gold is still hidden here in Murphys, but it is more likely that it was moved. The journal gives a record of Doc Strong and Smiley's travels to different locations on their way to the gold's final hiding place. The goal of our project is to follow Doc Strong's journey and study each site he mentioned in his journal.

"Now, I have to give you some bad news. You all were part of the project team at Villa Jovis and remember the problems we had with an archeologist named Bradford Damian. Although we could not prove it to the authorities, Damian made several attempts to steal valuable artifacts we discovered at the site. I have just discovered that he most likely will bring a crew to study the same sites we will be working at. He may offer to pay you a great deal of money for inside information or to steal artifacts for him. Be careful and report anything out of the ordinary to us. This man is a known black-market antiquities dealer. Working for him would ruin your career in archeology.

"Okay, it is time to get started. Dr. Kelly will meet with her team in front of the Murphys hotel, and I will meet my team at the site beside the Compere store building in fifteen minutes."

The teams walked in separate groups to their worksites, carrying their cameras, tools, and notebooks. Dan saw a black limousine parked behind the Murphys Hotel as they walked past the jailhouse. His team turned left onto Main Street and walked a few blocks to the Compere store building, stopping in a vacant lot to the right of the building.

Dan explained they were looking at the location of the miners' "Hall of Comparative Ovations." This was the Clampers' saloon and meeting hall. The building was specifically mentioned in Doc Strong's journal as the starting point of their travels. The building had burned down a decade later, and all that remained were a few of the foundation stones.

"I want you to do an extensive excavation of this site and document anything you find," he told his group. "After you finish this site, you will move next door to the Compere store building. This building was built in 1858 and has survived all of Murphys's many fires because of its thick walls and fireproof shutters. The building is now a private residence, and the owners are eager to have you study the building."

Kate met with her group in front of the Murphys hotel. She told her team that the hotel was opened in 1856 and was originally called the Sperry and Perry Hotel. "It is mentioned as the stage stop in Doc Strong's journal. The building has been remodeled several times, but the foundation and stone structure appear to be original. Make certain you look closely at the foundation and ask the hotel manager if there is any access to the area below the ground floor.

"When you finish your work on the Sperry Hotel, move to the Jones Apothecary building, kitty-corner across the street. Doctor Jones was a druggist and a close friend of Doc Strong. He was also a member of E Clampus Vitus. This building was built in 1856 and has been remodeled inside, but the limestone exterior structure is nearly original.

"In 1886, the building was opened as the 'Cheap Cash General Store,' and you can still see the old 'Cheap Cash' sign painted on the western wall of the building. Focus your attention on the building's foundation structure. Look for any sign of a basement storage area below ground level. Pharmacists usually would have a storage area below ground level to keep their stock of medicine cool during the hot summer months."

Dan walked up to Kate just as she was finishing with her team. They discussed the black limousine parked at the hotel as they walked down Algiers Road back to the campsite.

"I think we have a visitor, Dan."

"Yes, it looks like Veronica Bailey has arrived."

They walked back to the command tent, where they were met by Packard. "I found Damian nosing around the camp tents," he told them. They could see Bradford Damian sitting at one of the picnic tables, with one of Packard's undercover workers watching him. Dan said, "Good work, Jack."

As they approached Damian, Dan said, "I thought you learned a lesson in Capri. Stay away from my project camp."

Damian explained that he had only come to talk to them, and he was only looking in to the tents to find them.

"Nice try Damian; why are you really here?"

Damian told them Veronica Bailey wanted to have dinner with them that night at the Murphys Hotel. He explained that Bailey had set up her project headquarters at the hotel.

"Kate and I will stop by the hotel this afternoon. We need to set down some ground rules."

Dan then told Damian to leave the camp and report back to Bailey. Damian immediately left the camp and walked in the direction of the hotel. Dan and Kate went into Kate's tent and turned on her radio so they would not be overheard by anyone listening outside the tent. Dan asked Kate if she had brought Jim Smiley's cigar box. She took it out of her suitcase. Dan carefully inspected the carving on the outside of the box and could see the image of a gold miner panning for gold. He then looked inside of the box and saw a railroad scene, with a locomotive leaving a tunnel.

"Kate, I don't see anything that looks like a clue. You said there was a false bottom?"

Kate held the box and, after opening the lid, placed her fingers diagonally across two corners, and the false bottom popped up. She removed it, and Dan could see an area large enough to hide letters or a document. Kate told him that she had not found anything inside the false bottom when she first got the box. "I used it to hide letters you wrote me when were at school," she told him.

Dan chuckled. "That's not what I'm looking for, Kate."

Dan noticed that the underside of the removable false bottom was covered with an off-white paper that had started to curl up at the corner. He gave it a slight tug, and it dropped off, revealing the missing page from Doc Strong's journal. Kate was surprised she had not discovered the hidden page over the years she had used the box.

The page described Doc Strong's trip from Central Pacific Tunnel 3 above Cisco. He mentioned that Lewis Clement's crew was blasting at Tunnel 3 and Tunnel 4, and they could hear the tunnel blasts as they traveled around Big Bend and even when they reached the railroad camp at Mineral Spring House.

The journal mentioned their cargo for the first time. Doc Strong wrote that the mules carried twelve wooden barrels containing Judah's gold and the miners' gold that had been invested in Judah's project. After leaving the railroad camp, they went up the grade, where they were met by Lewis's team of Chinese tunnel workers. The workers placed the barrels in a cave-like vault and sealed the vault with a large granite door. The workers then gave Jim Smiley Judah's plumb bob and Doc

Strong a special spike that had been used to lock the granite door.

The journal then stated the men split up, with Clement and his workers traveling east to a work site outside of Tunnel 8. Doc Strong and Jim Smiley headed to Dutch Flat.

"Kate, this means the gold was hidden somewhere near Donner Pass."

Dan then noticed the number "1053" was written in pencil in the bottom corner of the page.

"I wonder what this number means?"

CHAPTER ELEVEN

Cave Hunting

Dan and Kate walked out of the tent into the deserted campsite and sat at a table near the creek. Dan opened John Richardson's notebook. The Pinkerton detective's notes were very detailed and described the pursuit of Doc Strong and an old miner, starting in Murphys. He wrote that he and the other detectives had searched the Murphys jailhouse and a hidden cavern about a mile out of town.

Whey found the cavern opening hidden behind a small shed, he was lowered about forty feet down to the floor of the cavern. The first thing he saw was about a half-dozen human skeletons directly below the opening. He then searched a series of cavern chambers and almost fell into a pit. He found fresh footprints and several circular scratches in the cavern floor, which he thought had been made by small barrels that had been stored in the cavern.

Richardson's notes also said that there were two separate sets of wagon tracks outside the cavern entrance. Richardson and his men followed the tracks headed in the direction of

Columbia. They lost the wagon tracks when they reached the river but continued on to Columbia, where they searched the town but did not find Doc Strong or the old redheaded miner.

Richardson and his men then rode back to Murphys, because he was convinced that there was a second wagon carrying gold from the cavern to Murphys. He found an empty freight wagon in Murphys but could not find its cargo. He attempted to question the miners in town but was unsuccessful at getting any information from the closed-mouthed prospectors. At this point, he knew that he had to move on if he had any hope of catching up to Doc Strong and the old miner.

Traveling back toward Sacramento, Richardson heard that a wagon with an old redheaded miner had passed through Sutter Creek the day before. The wagon was headed in the direction of Placerville. Richardson and his detectives then traveled to Placerville, where a merchant informed them that Doc Strong and a miner had bought supplies from his store about twelve hours earlier and then headed toward Coloma.

Richardson knew he was closing the gap between them and could travel much faster than the wagon. He traveled to Coloma but did not find Doc Strong or the miner. No one in the mining camp remembered seeing the wagon pass through the one-street town. Richardson decided the best road out of town headed to Auburn, and the wagon would have most likely taken that route.

Richardson and his men made good time to Auburn, but there was no trace of the wagon. He headed to the rail yards and met with a railroad foreman who had just come down the hill from Colfax. The foreman knew Doc Strong and said he had just seen him just outside Colfax, repairing a wagon wheel.

Richardson wasted no time. He raced to Colfax and arrived at the railroad camp just as a steam locomotive whistled and started its climb up to Cape Horn. In the distance, Richardson could see an old redheaded miner riding on a flat car at the end of the train. He asked a railroad worker where the train was headed and was told that it was headed to the railhead at Alta.

Richardson's horses were spent because of the hard ride, so he arranged for a fresh set of horses, and he and his men galloped uphill toward Alta. When they reached Alta, they could see the empty train on the track near the railroad camp, but there was no sign of Doc Strong or the miner.

Richardson stopped at a small cabin near the track and talked to Crocker's man James Strobridge, who said he had not seen Doc Strong. They walked with Strobridge to the railroad camp, and he asked one of the workmen if they had seen Doc Strong. The man told them that he might have seen him with a string of mules, riding up the railbed toward the tunnels near Donner Pass. Strobridge told Richardson that the fastest way to catch up to them would be to follow the river until just below Cisco, then ride uphill to the railroad right-of-way.

Richardson and his men wasted no time riding on the trail beside the river. When they reached a point below Cisco, they could see Doc Strong's mules, passing by the tunnel crews working on railroad Tunnel 3 and Tunnel 4.

They started the climb to Cisco, and all hell broke loose. The railroad workers starting blasting on both tunnel sites. Clouds of dust and rocks flew in their direction. After calming their horses, they finally climbed to the railroad camp at Cisco, where they were told they could not safely pass the tunnels until all the blasting was completed. Richardson helplessly watched as Doc Strong's mules traveled around the Big Bend curve and up the grade to Donner Pass.

Richardson knew it was useless to wait for the blasting to stop or try to catch them from the valley, so he returned to Murphys to see if he could track the location of the second wagon that had been at the hidden cave outside of town. He knew the odds of finding out what was loaded and where it was taken were slim, but he felt it was worth trying.

After a week of exploring Murphys and Angels Camp, he determined the second wagon must have carried the Clamper treasury, which included the "Carson Hill Gold Nugget" that weighed 160 pounds. He wrote in his journal that the Clamper treasury was already hidden in a safe place before he reached Murphys. Richardson ended the search and wrote Pinkerton's formal report on the investigation.

The report was delivered to James Bailey and the Associates in Sacramento. Richardson then left the Pinkerton detective agency and spent the next twenty years unsuccessfully searching for the lost Clamper gold hoard.

"Dan, this guy was serious about finding hidden gold here in Murphys."

Dan said, "It looks like we are looking for two hoards of gold—Judah's gold with the miners investment and the Clamper treasury."

Dan and Kate locked Richardson's journal in the jailhouse and walked to the Murphys Hotel to meet with Veronica Bailey. Dan asked the hotel clerk to call Bailey and tell her that they would be waiting for her in the hotel saloon. They then walked the few steps down the hallway and sat at a small table in the saloon to wait for Bailey.

Ten minutes later, Veronica Bailey arrived with Damian and sat down at their table. Bailey immediately said, "Welcome to Murphys."

She told them that she had a crew of experienced archeologists working for her in Murphys. She also told them that she already possessed information about the location of the lost Clamper Treasury and had enough information to know that Judah's gold was hidden somewhere near Donner Pass. She also told them it was only a matter of time before they found the gold without the help of Dan and Kate.

Dan looked at her and said, "I would not be so confident, Veronica; this a very complicated puzzle with many pieces required to find the exact location of Judah's gold."

"Yes, Dr. Strong, I am aware that you and Dr. Kelly have artifacts that I will need to locate and open the gold's hiding place. That is why I want to talk to you one last time. My offer to split the gold evenly still stands. I would consider this offer carefully, because I am not a patient person, and as you are aware I have the resources to get the artifacts away from you."

"Dr. Strong, you can't win this battle. I bet you were an eagle scout as a kid. Because you follow the rules, you're actions are predictable. The rules mean nothing to me, and give me an advantage that you can't overcome."

Dan told Bailey that her threats did not intimidate them, and they would not tolerate any interference with the University's project. He knew exactly what Damian was capable of doing and would immediately notify law enforcement of any attempts to interfere or steal any artifacts.

Bailey laughed and said, "Law enforcement? You mean FBI Special Agent Packard? He has bungled every investigation he has had on me. There is no way that he is a threat to me.

"I want an answer from you now. Will you cooperate with me and lead me to Judah's gold, or will I have to obtain the artifacts by myself?"

Dan looked at Kate. "There is no way that we will ever work with you to steal Judah's gold or any other historical artifacts. The answer is no!"

Kate and Dan got up from the table and left the saloon. They walked straight back to their tents at the project campsite. Dan found the box containing John Richardson's Colt Navy revolver and cleaned the gun. He then broke the seal on the powder flask and poured a small amount of the black powder on the table and held a match to it. There was a large flash, and a dense cloud of smoke filled the tent. Dan ran out of the tent for some fresh air and ran into Kate.

"What happened to your face? It looks like you have a blackface part in an old minstrel show. It is covered with black soot."

Dan wiped his face and said, "I just tested the black powder that came with Richardson's gun and discovered it still burns." Dan explained that he had not brought his gun that he usually carried at project sites, and in light of Bailey's threat, he thought it best to be armed against her goons.

Kate replied, "Why didn't you just ask me? I bought a new gun last week. You know I love to read adventure novels. I just read Ian Fleming's James Bond novel, *Dr. No,* and I decided I wanted a nifty little Walther PPK just like James Bond used." Dan shook his head and laughed. "Okay, secret agent, you hold onto it. You may need it for protection."

Dan went back into the tent and carefully loaded the antique revolver and placed the percussion caps in place on the cylinder. He tucked the gun into his pants and walked out to the campsite. Outside the tent, Kate took a quick look at him and said, "Either you are very happy to see me, or you have a gun tucked into your family jewels."

Dan looked down the slid the gun around to his side. "Thanks, Kate, that could have been real painful."

Dan then told Kate they should check out the cavern where the gold was originally hidden. They got into Dan's car and drove a short distance out of Murphys to the parking lot for Mercer Caverns. They paid their admission and were given a small brochure that provided the history of the cavern and a map of the layout. Before they went down the wooden staircase, Kate said, "There is something I don't understand. The brochure said the cavern was discovered in 1885, about twenty-two years after the miners hid the gold in the cavern."

Dan explained that the cavern was discovered by native Indians decades or even centuries before 1885 and used as a burial chamber. During the gold rush, the miners literally looked under every rock for gold and would have found it as well. The Clampers probably covered the cavern opening after they moved their gold, and its location was lost over time.

Dan looked at the brochure and read that the entrance that they were using to enter the cave was not the original entrance to the cave. The owners of the cavern had excavated a new entrance and used the original entrance as an exit.

They descended into the cavern on a wooden staircase and walked through several chambers in the cavern. Dan said, "We need to find the area that is below the original entrance to the cavern."

After walking through a couple of chambers, they found the second set of wooden steps and looked up to see the opening about forty feet above their heads.

"Okay, Kate, we are directly below the original opening. Look for a small area where they could have hidden the barrels."

They found a small area off what was called the "Gothic Chamber" that could have been used to store the barrels. As they looked closely at the floor, they could see a series of circular scratches in the floor, like the ones described in Richardson's notebook.

"We found it, Dan." After looking at the cavern floor Kate tried to photograph the rings. Just as the camera flashed, a gunshot echoed through the cavern, and a cloud of white dust went in the air as a bullet hit the wall of the cave beside Dan.

They rushed behind a large pillar and heard a voice echo through the cavern. "Dr. Strong, throw out your gun. You are in a no win situation. I can see you, but you can't see me." After a short silence the voice said, "I do not wish to harm you or your partner, but I only need one of you to give me information on the gold that was hidden in this cave."

Dan answered, "We don't know where the gold was taken." The voice replied, "Don't act dumb, you have information and items that we need to find the gold, and I only need one of you to give it to me."

Another gunshot was heard, and it shattered a stalagmite beside Kate. The voice said, that was just a warning, I am an excellent shot and Dr. Kelly is in my gun sight." Dan moved in front of Kate to shield her, and whispered, "I have an idea Kate. Follow me to the staircase when I fire the gun. Keep your gun ready in case you need to use it."

Dan cocked the revolver and jumped toward the staircase. The gun flashed and spewed a huge black cloud of dense smoke, obscuring the gunman's vision. Kate followed Dan through the dense smoke, while Dan fired three shots in the direction of the gunman's voice. They climbed the staircase and exited the cave before the gunman could get another shot at them.

Dan told Kate to watch out for other gunmen, as their eyes were adjusting to the sunlight. They saw Packard standing at the cave opening, and he told them to stand behind the ticket building while his men flushed out the shooter. He then pointed a bullhorn at the entrance of the cave and said, "This is the FBI! Drop your gun and leave the cave with your arms raised. Don't try anything stupid; you have no way out."

A man came up the exit staircase with his hands raised, and he was handcuffed as he left the cave. Packard asked the gunman if there was anyone else inside the cave, and he said he was alone. Several agents carefully entered both entrances to the cave and searched the cavern and returned about ten minutes later. One of the agents told Packard the cave was clear, and they had found the weapon on the cave floor.

Dan looked at Packard and asked, "How did you get here so quickly?"

A smiling Packard replied, "I followed you here, when you left the camp, without telling me where you were going."

CHAPTER TWELVE

Eureka!

Dan and Kate drove straight back to the campsite and talked about their ambush in the cavern. Dan told Kate, "Bailey is definitely playing hardball and will strike again soon. I do not know if she is still trying to scare us off, or if she really wants to eliminate us." After a few minutes, they relaxed and laughed about the cloud of smoke and the sound of cannon fire that came out of the old pistol.

"Kate, you have to agree that it was very effective diversion."

They laughed and walked to the campsite kitchen filled their plates, and sat down at a table near the creek. Kate mentioned that she was amazed the barrel rings were still there, just as described in Richardson notebook. Dan said, "Richardson's notes were so accurate that I also believe that a Clamper treasury, separate from their investment in the railroad, really was hidden here in Murphys. Bailey mentioned the Clamper treasury when we talked to her today, and she probably knew about it because of the Pinkerton report that was given to James Bailey in 1863."

Dan and Kate could see the students gathering for a meeting, so they finished their meal and went to meet with their teams.

Kate gave her team their next assignment. She asked them to complete their survey of the Jones Apothecary building and then to start work on the old Fisk building. She told them that this building was originally built in 1859 as the Union Saloon and Bowling Alley and had burned down at least two times. One of the students told Kate that they had met with the storeowner of the Jones Apothecary, and he told them that there was no basement. The storeowner even removed a section of flooring so they could look at the foundation. He gave them an old prescription logbook that dated back to 1863. The student also told her that the team was also given Dr. Jones's journal, which had been stored in the building since the gold rush days.

Dan assigned the Traver building to his team and explained that it was the oldest building in Murphys, and was currently being used as an automotive garage.

Dan and Kate then walked to the headquarters tent with the prescription log and Dr. Jones's journal. The prescription log was a leather bound book with paper prescriptions pasted to the pages. Kate paged through the journal and said, "Dan, Jones was the Clamper treasurer, and this log contains their income and expenses for a five-year period—from 1862 to 1867."

The society's major source of income was the from the initiation of new members, whom they called PBCs (for "Poor

Blind Candidates"). The initiation fee to the miner brother-hood was typically one poke of gold dust. It also listed their expenses for whiskey and spirits, major expenses for building a schoolhouse, and support money for widows of miners in the area.

"Dan, look at this!" Kate showed him an entry for the with-drawal of more than three hundred thousand dollars of gold dust and gold nuggets from the cave. The journal also stated that the rest of the treasury and the Carson Hill Nugget tem-porarily were moved to a Wells Fargo building in Douglas Flat, where they were guarded twenty-four hours a day until it was hidden in Murphys, in the ice storage basement of the Union Saloon and Bowling Alley.

"Kate, let's go check go check the progress at the old Fisk building."

They walked to the jailhouse and locked the prescription log and Dr. Jones's journal in the back cell of the building, then walked to the old Fisk building. Kate checked the progress of her students; they had already photographed and measured the exte-rior of the building. One student told her that the building had been rebuilt several times, and the exterior stonework was a dif-ferent pattern than seen in the other buildings in Murphys. They had already pulled up some of the floorboards inside the building and had found an unusual pattern of large, flat rectangular stones that could be covering a small basement area. They also had dis-covered that one stone had "ECV 1866" chiseled into the granite.

The owner of the building approached Dan and told him that he had just received an offer to purchase the building from Veronica Bailey. Dan told him that he would match the offer and pay the storeowner a finder's fee if anything of value was found under the building. The storeowner told Dan he had been trying to sell the building for years, and now he had gotten two offers in the same day. He shook hands with Dan.

"It's a deal."

Dan then said, "We need to work quickly, before Bailey hears about this."

Jack Packard arrived at the store, and Kate gave him an update on the possible discovery of the hiding place of the Clamper treasury.

"Kate, you mean there are two sites with gold?"

She explained that the gold that might be under this building was the treasury that remained after the miners removed their investment in the railroad. She also told him that there also might be a 160-pound gold nugget as well.

"Wait a minute, Dan. This is our chance to catch Bailey in the act of stealing the gold." Packard explained that they needed to leak the discovery to Bailey and give her an opportunity to steal the big gold nugget. He would then catch her in the act of stealing valuable historical artifacts.

Dan didn't like the sound of this. He told Packard they would be endangering extremely important and valuable treasure without any guarantee of catching Bailey or her crew of black-market thieves.

"You're wrong, Dan; this time her arrogance will be her downfall," Packard replied. "That huge gold nugget is a trophy she cannot resist. My experience with her says she will steal it as soon as it is possible. The FBI believes she has her own private museum, securely hidden in the sub-basement of her San Francisco mansion or possibly at another location. Our requests for a search warrant for her San Francisco mansion have been turned down in the past, but if we can track the movement of the stolen gold nugget to her home, we will have more than enough evidence to get a search warrant. When we find her treasure trove of stolen art and valuable artifacts, we'll finally have enough evidence to put her away for a very long time."

Packard then described his plan to catch Bailey. His agents would place a small radio transmitter in a transport box they would build for the large gold nugget and a smaller transmitter in the packing material that wrapped the nugget. "We will store the nugget in the old jailhouse, and I am certain Bailey will break in to the jail and take the nugget before the armored car can get there to transport it to Stanford. We can then track the nugget to her hidden trophy room. If anything goes wrong, we will immediately arrest the people transporting the gold nugget."

"It would be fantastic if your men could catch Veronica Bailey," Dan mused. "She is a constant threat to Kate and me."

Dan and three team members used large pry bars to lift a granite stone below the floorboards. They moved the stone to the side, and Dan used his flashlight to look into the basement area below. Suddenly he shouted, "Eureka!"

He immediately lowered a ladder into the basement and shone his light on a large, flat quartz rock that sparkled a bright golden color.

"Kate, come down here with the Graflex camera. You have to see this."

Kate climbed down the ladder and shone her spotlight around the room. She could see the glistening gold nugget and rows of wooden barrels stacked around the perimeter of the basement. She handed the camera to one of the students to take photographs of the location of all the items in the room. The student first placed paper numbers on each item, then shot a series of photographs to document their location in the room. Dan removed the lids of several of the barrels and confirmed they contained gold nuggets or gold dust in leather pokes. He estimated that each of the forty barrels contained over two hundred pounds of gold.

Dan and Kate then climbed out of the basement and told Packard that there were four tons ton of gold dust and nuggets in the basement that need to be moved to a safe place immediately. They also told him that the Carson Hill nugget was there as well.

Packard told them he needed to make a few phone calls to arrange for transportation and storage of the gold. He returned a few minutes later and told Kate and Dan that he had made arrangements to move the gold to the San Francisco Mint. He said, "There is an army unit conducting training exercises nearby that will transport the gold with a full military escort to the Mint. They have their orders and should arrive within an hour." Packard told them he had also arranged for an armored car to take the gold nugget to Stanford in the morning. "That should give Bailey enough time to try to steal the gold nugget from the jailhouse."

Dan called the students together for a meeting and informed them of what was going to happen. "We will study their contents after our fieldwork is completed," he said. "The Carson Hill nugget will be shipped by armored car to Stanford in the morning."

Kate then gave both teams their instructions for preparing the barrels for shipping. Each barrel would be sealed with a tamper-resistant band and then wrapped in a canvas bag to prevent loss of the contents, in case the barrel broke in transit. There also were two large ice tongs in the basement that would be stored with the other artifacts that were found in Murphys.

Dan noticed Damian lurking on the sidewalk outside the old Fisk building, listening to their meeting. Dan waited a few minutes to make certain that he had heard the plans for moving the Carson Hill nugget, then went out the front door of the building said, "Damian, keep moving along; there is nothing here that concerns you or your boss."

Damian then walked down Main Street to the Murphys Hotel. Dan told Kate and Packard that Damian had taken the bait.

The students wrapped the large nugget with the shipping blanket containing the transmitter and placed it into the wooden box the FBI had prepared. Dan looked at the blanket and saw the outline of the radio transmitter. "Jack," he said, "the transmitter in the blanket is too obvious. Bailey will see it and know we are tracking the nugget."

Dan took out his pocketknife and carefully removed the transmitter and gave it to Kate, who placed it in her pocket and went back to work with the students. An hour later, a group of army transport trucks drove up to the building and loaded the barrels onto two of the trucks. Four soldiers armed with Thompson machine guns climbed in the back of each truck. There was a lead car and jeeps before and after each truck in the convoy of vehicles that left Murphys.

The students carried the wooden box containing the Carson Hill nugget to the old jailhouse and locked the large iron doors, while Kate and Dan returned to their tents.

Packard went into Dan's tent, and they discussed their plans for following the gold nugget when it was stolen. Packard said two of the FBI cars were equipped with a tracking device to follow the radio signal from the wooden box. The agents would need to stay within two miles of the transmitter to get a clear signal.

CHAPTER THIRTEEN

Kidnapped

While Dan and Packard were talking, Kate decided she needed to review John Richardson's notes for additional clues to the location of Judah's gold. The notes were locked in the back of the jailhouse. She did not think that Bailey's men had time to act yet, so she walked to the old jailhouse. As she unlocked the doors and went into the jailhouse, she heard the sound of a truck stop outside the building, and suddenly two men grabbed her. She put up a fight and screamed until they gagged her and threw her into the back of the truck. They then took the Carson Hill nugget out of the box and placed in the back of the delivery truck with Kate.

Dan and Packard heard Kate scream. As they ran out of the tent, they saw Kate being thrown into the back of the truck, followed by three men carrying a large object that looked like the nugget. Dan grabbed his bag and Kate's gun as he ran to his car to follow the truck. As he started the car, he said, "Jack, Kate has the radio transmitter in her pocket. I am going to follow the truck so we don't lose it, but get your tracking units on the road."

Dan then stomped on the accelerator of the Buick and raced after the truck. He saw the FBI agents scramble into their cars in his rearview mirror. The Buick caught up to the truck, but suddenly a car came from a side street and opened fire on him, shattering a side window.

Dan backed off the truck and continued to follow from a distance when one of the FBI cars sped by him and shot out the tires of the truck's escort vehicle, which ran off the road and hit a tree. The FBI car then fell back and followed the truck from a distance. The truck was headed toward Columbia, and a few miles after crossing a bridge, it turned into the entrance of the Columbia airport.

Dan could see Veronica Bailey's limousine near a twin-engine Executive Lodestar, warming up on the edge of the runway. The truck drove beside the limousine, and two of the men carried Kate into the plane, kicking them every step of the way. The men returned to the truck and carried the large nugget toward the plane.

Dan drove past the first FBI car and stopped his car in front of the plane. He then ran toward the entrance to the plane and pointed Kate's gun at the men as they moved the nugget. Suddenly, gunshots came from the door of the plane, narrowly missing Dan. He took cover behind the truck as the men loaded the nugget into the baggage compartment of the plane. Three of the men, carrying machine guns, came out of the plane as the propellers started to spin. The men released the brakes of Dan's car and pushed it out of the way.

Dan tried to get into position to shoot the plane's front wheel, but the three men pinned him down as they boarded the plane. The plane moved onto the runway, with one gunman firing from the doorway. The twin engine plane took off, heading east.

Dan walked back to where Packard was standing and said, "Thanks a lot, Jack! Bailey got away with Kate. We have to find out where she is taking her."

"Don't worry, Dan. We will find out where they are headed and catch her when they land at their destination."

They walked to the airport office and asked to see the flight plan for the plane. The manager told them the flight plan listed New York City's LaGuardia Airport as the destination and did not list any intermediate refueling stops.

"That's not good enough, Jack; she may diverge from the flight plan and land at a totally different destination."

Dan asked the airport manager if there were any charter planes available at the airport. He replied, "There is a charter pilot warming up for a flight to Denver, and he may have room for you. You could then transfer to one of the new commercial jets in Denver and might be able to arrive at LaGuardia before the Lodestar."

Dan and Jack walked to a bright red Cessna 195 that was warming up its huge rotary engine. The pilot waved them into the plane, and after a short conversation, he agreed to take him to Denver's Stapleton Airport.

"Okay, Dan, I will have an agent meet you in Denver with a ticket for a flight to New York City. I also will have agents covering every airport in the New York City area, just in case she changes airports."

Dan took his seat in the plane, and the pilot took off down the runway and lifted off. The plane had left the airport about fifteen minutes behind Bailey. The pilot told Dan that Bailey's twin-engine Lodestar was slightly faster than his single-engine Cessna 195, but Dan should beat the Lodestar to New York on the commercial jet.

Dan explained the reason for his flight to the pilot, who made arrangements by radio to park his plane near the commercial airport gates.

The plane hit air turbulence, and Dan grimaced and closed his eyes. The pilot asked him if he had ever flown before. Dan told him that he used to fly a lot, but had had a very bad experience flying in Egypt when his plane crash-landed in the Nile.

Dan looked at the peaks of the mountains beside the plane, and said, "Whoa! What are you doing?"

The pilot grinned and said, "Don't worry Dan, I have a great deal of experience flying through these mountain passes. Just sit back and enjoy the scenery."

An FBI agent met the plane when they reached Denver. He introduced himself as Special Agent Charles Chambers and gave Dan a ticket for a Boeing 707 that was departing for New York in ten minutes. Dan ran up the boarding ramp to the plane just as they were closing the aircraft door and took his seat. The plane rolled out of the terminal on schedule.

As the plane taxied to the runway, Dan saw Bailey's plane being fueled at a distant part of the airport. At first, Dan was upset he had not noticed the plane when he landed, but then realized he would not have had the resources or support necessary to stop her anyway. He knew he would have had to rely on the support of only one FBI agent, and that would not have been enough to overcome Bailey's well-armed guards.

The flight to New York City was smooth, and Dan slept most of the trip. The plane reached LaGuardia Airport early in the morning, and Special Agent James Sperry met him. Sperry told Dan that he and his men were assigned to follow Veronica Bailey to her final destination and to stop her when they had enough evidence to arrest her in the act of stealing valuable objects. Dan said, "Why don't you just arrest her for kidnapping Kate Kelly as soon as the plane arrives?"

Sperry told Dan, "My orders come directly from FBI Director Hoover, and he wants to find all the art treasures she has stolen around the world. We will arrest her for kidnapping if we don't find her collection of stolen art treasures at her destination."

Dan asked Sperry if he knew when Bailey's plane would arrive and was told it would land in an hour. The plane would be directed to an empty gate at the end of the terminal building. The two baggage handlers at the gate were FBI agents, as was the taxi coordinator at the cabstand. FBI agents were driving the first two taxis at the taxi stand, and there were three FBI cars waiting in case a limousine picked Bailey up. They would follow her to her destination.

Dan asked, "How can I help?"

"It would be helpful if you could identify Veronica Bailey and Dr. Kelly when they get off the plane." Sperry looked at Dan's work clothes and added that he would have to change in into a suit to avoid being noticed. They walked to Sperry's car, and he pulled a suit jacket, slacks, and shirt out of a suitcase in his trunk. "I always keep a spare when I work in the field."

Dan walked into the terminal and changed into the suit; then he bought a tie with a bright red apple logo from the airport gift shop. Sperry walked up to him and chuckled. "Nice tie, Dr. Strong. No one will confuse you with an FBI agent."

Sperry told Dan that the plane was early and on final approach to the airport. They walked to the airport tarmac and stood behind a baggage cart near the plane's arrival gate. Bailey's plane arrived at the gate ten minutes later, and the aircraft door opened as soon as the propellers stopped. Bailey and Kate got off the plane, closely followed by one of Bailey's guards, who appeared to have a gun pushed up against Kate's back. Dan said, "The black-haired woman is definitely Veronica Bailey, and the redhead is my partner, Katherine Kelly."

Sperry radioed his men that they had a positive identification of Veronica Bailey and the kidnapping victim.

The undercover baggage handlers took all the luggage except for a blanket-covered object, which was pushed to the taxi stand on a baggage cart by two of Bailey's guards. The taxi coordinator was told they needed two taxis, and they were headed to 405 Lexington Avenue. He whistled for two taxis. Bailey, Kate, and a guard got in the first cab, and the two other guards rode in the second cab with the baggage and the heavy, blanket-wrapped object.

Sperry walked up to the taxi coordinator, who told him where the cabs were headed. Sperry said, "That address seems very familiar for some reason."

THE CHRYSLER BUILDING

Photo by Carol Highsmith

CHAPTER FOURTEEN

Climbing the Chrysler Building

Dan and Sperry got into Sperry's car and followed Bailey's taxis into Manhattan to their destination and watched them leave the taxi and enter the building. Dan looked at the angular black marble entrance, then looked skyward and said, "Holy crap! This the Chrysler Building."

Sperry told Dan, "Tracking Bailey is going to be difficult. The building has thirty-two elevators and the population of a small city. I already have two agents in the building; I hope they can determine where they are going."

Dan immediately jumped out the car so he would not lose track of Kate and Bailey's entourage. He entered the three-story, triangular lobby and walked toward the four banks of elevators and saw Bailey, Kate, and one of the guards entered an elevator in the middle. When he reached the elevator, he watched the control panel on the marble wall, noting that the elevator traveled to the sixty-ninth floor.

Sperry entered the lobby and went straight to Dan. "Did you see where they went?"

"Yes, the elevator went to the sixty-ninth floor."

Sperry told Dan that he already had stationed men at the three main lobby entrances and had men watching all of the elevators. He added that he would raid the sixty-ninth floor from the elevator and staircases above and below when he had enough men.

Dan told Sperry that he was not going to wait for the raid; he would go up and scout the sixty-ninth floor. Sperry replied, "It's not going to be that easy, Dan. The building supervisor just told me that the sixty-ninth floor used to be Walter Chrysler's private gymnasium, and elevator service is restricted on the sixty-ninth and seventieth floors, requiring a special key once the elevator reaches the floor. Anyone accessing these floors would activate a doorbell that would announce their arrival to the occupants of those floors.

"Damn, there has got to be a way to get there undetected," Dan replied. Then he noticed a sign for the Cloud Club on the sixty-sixth floor and asked Sperry about the club. Sperry told him that the Cloud Club was built as a '30s-era speakeasy for the New York elite. "Today, it is an exclusive men-only membership club for New York City's tycoons and executives. It has a lounge and grill on the sixty-sixth floor and a private dining room and restaurant on the sixty-seventh and sixty-eighth floors."

"How do I get in the club?" Dan asked.

Sperry told him that the club was very strict and would only admit members and their guests.

Dan remembered reading about Juan Trippe, the president of Pan American Airlines, in a magazine during his flight to New York City. He guessed that Trippe certainly would be a member of the Cloud Club.

"See you at the top, James."

Dan then walked to a center elevator and rode it to sixty-sixth-floor entrance to the Cloud Club. He walked up to maître d' at a desk in front of the elevator and he said he was there to meet with Juan Trippe of Pan American Airlines. The maître d' told him Mr. Trippe was already in the private dining room, but he had not mentioned having a visitor today. Dan told him Trippe had called him bring him information on a problem with a flight to South America.

The maître d' told Dan that Mr. Trippe often forgot to notify him of guests and that he could take the staircase up to the private dining room.

Dan walked by the Tudor-style lounge and the Old English Grill Room before he climbed the bronze and marble staircase to the sixty-seventh floor. He walked past the private dining room and entered the main dining room. Dan was surprised how small the main dining room was.

He found a service staircase in a corner of the room and climbed the stairs to the sixty-ninth floor. He carefully opened the door and saw a tall, continuous open space surrounded by triangular windows and a staircase leading to the seventieth floor. The walls in between the windows were covered with priceless works of art, and there were sculptures and display cases containing gold coins spaced around the room.

He then saw Kate, sitting on a cluster of lounge seats in the center of the room, with her hands tied and a gag on her mouth. He ran to her side and used his pocketknife to cut the rope that bound her hands and pulled off her gag. Kate whispered, "Be careful, they just went up the stairs to Bailey's apartment."

"Let's get out of here, Kate. It looks like we have found Bailey's trophy room."

They were headed toward the service staircase when they heard Veronica Bailey say, "What a marvelous surprise! I now have both of you as my guests."

They looked up at the staircase and saw Bailey and three of her guards. The guards ran down the stairs with their guns pointed at Dan and Kate. Dan pulled out Kate's gun, pointed it at Bailey, and said, "Shoot me, and your boss will get a bullet through her heart. Drop your guns and lie on the floor."

The three guards stopped and looked up at Bailey. She said, "Drop the guns, and follow his directions."

The three men dropped their guns and lay down on the floor. Kate collected their guns and ran to Dan's side. They both started up the stairs to where Bailey was standing.

Dan told Bailey to go up the stairs, and she slowly walked up the steps and entered the apartment. She then slammed and locked the door behind her, leaving Dan and Kate stranded on the staircase. All three angry guards pulled a second back-up gun from their jackets.

Dan shot the lock off the door, and they ran into the apartment but could not see Bailey. They looked across the living room and saw the elevator door. They crossed the room and pressed the button for the elevator, and there was no response.

Kate and Dan then ran across the apartment to a formal dining area and entered the adjoining kitchen. Inside the kitchen they saw the access door to the service stairs, and they ran up to the stairs to the seventy-first floor. Dan looked around and said, "This used to be the Chrysler building's public observation deck, and it had an express elevator for the tourists. Hopefully it still works."

They found the elevator and pressed the button, but it did not light up. Dan said, "Give me a break! They must have deactivated the elevator call system to prevent unwanted visitors."

Dan and Kate could hear Bailey's gunmen on the stairs below them, and after a minute of searching, they found another fire staircase in the building's central core.

"Kate, we have no choice; we have to go up."

They were surprised to discover that the staircase was not straight; they climbed eight steps north, two steps east, and five steps south. The fifteen concrete steps brought them to a brick-walled landing that was marked with the number 72. There was no floor, only a landing leading to more stairs.

They went up another fifteen steps and arrived at a similar landing, marked 73. There still was no floor, so they went up another three steps and went through an unmarked door. They could see a floor with a large water storage tank and two large elevator motors. On all sides they could see trapezoidal portions of three large triangular windows that rose from below the floor.

Dan locked the metal door they had just passed through and said, "We need to slow Bailey's thugs down, so that Sperry's agents can catch up."

They climbed a few more steps to the seventy-fourth floor, walked past four banks of electrical transformers, and found a pegboard-covered office with a sign labeled "WPAT-FM Radio." The office was dark and unoccupied. Dan entered the office, where he immediately found the telephone and called the building manager's number listed on the phone. When he was connected to the office, he told them to get an emergency message to FBI agent Sperry that Kate and Dan were on the seventy-fourth floor and were being chased by gunmen. While he was still speaking, they heard a gunshot coming from the floor below them and ran out of the office.

"They must have blown the lock off the door, Kate. Let's keep climbing."

They ran up the next fifteen steps of the fire staircase to the doorway to the seventy-fifth floor, which they entered and locked behind them. They could see clouds outside the building and noticed the triangular windows no longer had glass panes and were open to the elements. The wind sounded loud as it blew across the floor.

They found another stairway and climbed twenty-three more steps to the seventy-sixth floor, where the wind temporarily quieted down. Dan and Kate felt like they had stepped into a mountain cave. The tips of the triangular windows barely peeked through the floor. The area was dark, tucked into the upper reaches of the fourth arch of the building's spire. Dan looked around and discovered they had reached the end of the staircase; there was only one way to go—up.

They climbed small steel ladder, less than one foot in width, to the seventy-seventh floor. Dan followed Kate up the twenty-two rungs, and they emerged into a brightly lit area surrounded by three window openings. The view was like what Dan had seen from the airliner at cruising altitude, except a high wind rushed through the open windows. Dan looked up and saw that the next ladder was even narrower than the one they had just climbed.

"Stay here; I want to see what the next floor looks like," Dan said. He quickly climbed the steps to a small landing, and he could see that he had reached the beginning of the needle on top of the Chrysler building's spire. The ladder went up about eight additional floors in the narrow needle. He then returned to Kate and said, "There is no use going any higher. There is nowhere to hide from them up there."

Dan looked around the floor and saw a roll of heavy industrial cable that must have been used for the radio transmitters.

"Kate, I have an idea, but I know you will not like it."

He tied one end of the cable to a building column near a window and tied the other end to Kate and himself. They heard the gunfire of the Bailey's men blowing the lock off the door on the seventy-fifth floor.

"Enjoy the ride, Kate."

Kate looked at the open widow and said, "Oh, my God!"

Dan and Kate climbed out the window and Dan lowered them down the stainless steel skin of the Chrysler building's spire to an open window on the seventy-fifth floor, where they dangled 868 feet above the street below. Dan and Kate hung suspended above Manhattan for a few minutes, but it seemed like hours. Dan waited until the gunmen had gone up the stairs to the seventy-sixth floor; then he helped Kate into the building and followed her.

Kate whispered furiously, "Don't ever do that again!"

They quickly untied the cable and ran back down the staircase to Bailey's trophy room on the sixty-ninth floor, where they ran into Sperry and his men. Dan informed Sperry that the gunmen were up in the higher floors of the building with no way to escape. He also told him that that they had lost track of Veronica Bailey in her apartment.

Sperry directed his men to search the upper floors of the building to flush out the gunmen. He returned to the trophy room about thirty minutes later and told Dan they had Bailey's men in custody, but there was no sign of Veronica Bailey.

WALDORF ASTORIA HOTEL

Photo by James G. Howes

CHAPTER FIFTEEN

Life at the Waldorf

Kate and Dan walked around Bailey's trophy room with Sperry, identifying many of the priceless paintings and sculptures in Bailey's collection of stolen art. They told him that many of them were national treasures stolen from museums around the world. They found the Carson Hill nugget in a corner of the room and told Sperry that Bailey had just stolen it from their archeology project in California. They also found an entire group of paintings Bailey had stolen from New York City's Museum of Modern Art. Dan said, "Veronica Bailey has to be extremely pissed off that she just lost a collection that took years to steal."

Sperry said, "Yes, and if she escapes, she will be out for revenge, and you two will be the target of her anger."

He took a key to the elevator out of his pocket. "Let's go down to the lobby and see if my men managed to catch Bailey trying to escape from the building."

They rode the fast tower elevator to the fifty-seventh floor, where Sperry checked with his agents searching the building. The lead agent reported that they had not seen Bailey. They then took the express elevator to the lobby. They walked out of the elevator, and an agent walked up to Sperry and said, "Boss, I have bad news. Veronica Bailey was observed leaving the basement level of the building and entering the Lexington Avenue subway station before we had our men in place."

Sperry told them that Bailey must have had a preplanned escape route for an emergency. "I will notify security at all the airports and train stations, but the chances of catching her are not good."

Sperry asked Dan if there was a safe place he could take them. Dan told him that they had not made any arrangements, as this trip definitely was not planned. Sperry told him that it was difficult to get last minute hotel reservations in Manhattan, but he thought he could get them a room in the safest place in New York City. He told them that he had a friend at the Waldorf Astoria who might be able to help out. "We often use the Waldorf when we have high-profile visitors to the city whom we need to protect," he told them.

They walked out to the street, got into Sperry's car, and drove to the 49th Street entrance to the Waldorf Astoria's parking garage. As they turned into the garage, Sperry pointed out a polished brass garage door and told them, "That is the door to an elevator that goes down to the Waldorf's private railroad siding, which we have used on occasion to get dignitaries out of the hotel without being seen. When FDR was president, he used it when his private railroad car, the *Ferdinand Magellan*, came to town. The Secret Service would transfer him from the private railcar to his Pierce Arrow automobile in the elevator so the public would not see the results of his polio. We call it Track 61, and it is totally isolated from the hotel. The only way down to the siding is through the elevator and two fire escape staircases that are not connected to the hotel."

Sperry parked his car near the entrance to the hotel lobby, and they walked through the ornate central lobby past a large bronze clock topped by a model of the Statue of Liberty and an American eagle. As they walked, Sperry told them that they were going to meet Sean O'Brian, the hotel's head of security. "O'Brian is a retired New York City police officer and quite a character. He loves his Irish heritage and will definitely love you, Dr. Kelly."

They stopped at the Hilton Towers desk near the 50th Street side of the building, and Sperry asked to see Sean O'Brian. They waited about five minutes, and then a tall man with red hair walked up to Sperry and said, "Top of the day to you, my friend. How can I help you today?"

Sperry introduced Kate and Dan to him and explained that they had just helped the FBI break up a black market art operation and would need a safe place to stay for the next couple of days. O'Brian looked at Kate and said, "Of course I will help this beautiful colleen and her friend."

O'Brian walked to the Waldorf Towers desk, spoke briefly to the hotel manager, and returned with a key to a room in the Waldorf Towers. He then escorted all of them to one of the Tower elevators, and they rode it to the forty-second floor. As they rode the elevator O'Brian said, "Security is extremely tight for the protection of our guests in the Waldorf Towers suites. The official residence of the United States' Permanent

Representative to the United Nations, is located on the same floor as your suite."

They exited the elevator and walked past a door with a United Nations Seal to a doorway down the hall that said 42B. O'Brian opened the door to the penthouse suite, and they saw a beautiful white marble entranceway that led to a living room complete with two sofas and a grand piano. O'Brian showed them the bedrooms and a large, formal dining room.

O'Brian then asked if they had any baggage, and Dan said, "This trip was totally unexpected; we did not have a chance to take any luggage."

"I will see what I can do for you," O'Brian replied.

O'Brian and Sperry then walked out of suite toward the elevator. Dan and Kate could hear Sperry fill O'Brian in on this case, as they walked.

Dan closed the door after them, and he and Kate wandered through the six-thousand-square-foot penthouse. The living areas were all off-white with gold trim. They looked through the windows and could see three different views of the Manhattan skyline outside and St. Bartholomew's Church below them on 50th Street.

"This place is unbelievable, Dan," said Kate.

Dan told her, "Sperry picked the Waldorf for a reason. He knows Bailey's background, and she is going to be gunning for us after losing her art treasures. This is a pretty big case for the FBI, and the last thing they want is to have their witnesses shot after helping them. The security in the Waldorf Towers is formidable. There are only two elevators, and the fire staircases are closely monitored to prevent unwanted visitors."

Dan and Kate heard a doorbell ring at the back service entrance to the suite, and a maid entered.

"Good afternoon. I will be one of the maids taking care of your suite during your stay."

The maid was carrying fresh towels, cotton bathrobes, and toiletries for Kate and Dan. She placed all of the items in two of the bathrooms and returned to where they were standing.

"Please feel free to call me, using the maid call buttons, if there is anything you need for your room."

The telephone rang; it was Jack Packard, back at the Murphys dig site.

"Hello, Dan. Congratulations on finding Bailey's collection of stolen art. There are museums around the world celebrating the finding of their priceless art. I am sorry that you and Kate were put in danger. God, I heard that you even had to jump out of a window on the top of the Chrysler Building to escape from Bailey's men. It's too bad that Bailey got away. You two will have to be extremely careful; she will try to take revenge on you two."

Packard told Dan he had kept an eye of the graduate students, and they had done a fantastic job. They had finished the Murphys site ahead of schedule and were ready to move the camp to Alta."

"Jack, have the team leaders give us a call."

"Sure, Dan. I have to go now, but make sure you watch out for Bailey's men. She has to be mad as a hornet and looking to get back at you."

Dan hung up the phone and told Kate that everything was going well at the dig. Kate said, "I cannot believe how much has happened to us in one day. When will we be able to fly home and get back to work?"

"Fly home? No way, Kate! I do not fly. The only reason I flew here was because I was desperate to get you out of danger."

Dan told Kate about his flight to New York City.

He told Kate she was welcome to fly home, but he would take the train back to California. Kate agreed they should stay together and take the train. During the trip, they would have to keep their eyes open for Bailey's men.

The phone rang. It was the project leaders, calling to give their updates to Dan and Kate. Kate talked to both team leaders and then told them to go ahead and move their camp to the new site at Alta. She thanked both leaders for keeping the project on track and told them they would see Dan and her in a week.

The telephone rang again, and it was the hotel concierge. He told Dan that Mr. O'Brian had asked him to contact two clothiers to bring a selection of clothing up to their room, as their luggage had not arrived at the hotel. The concierge also told him that they would be receiving an invitation from the Waldorf to have dinner in the Empire Room and to enjoy a special performance by Louis Armstrong at nine-thirty that night.

The doorbell to the suite rang a few minutes later. Dan opened the door, and there was a tailor and seamstress in the hallway, each pulling a cart with clothing and a small suitcase. Dan let them into the suite. The seamstress went with Kate to her bedroom, and Kate tried on several evening dresses. She found a beautiful black evening dress that was a perfect fit right off the rack. She also selected a casual travel outfit that the seamstress said she would adjust and bring back within an hour. She also gave Kate a selection of undergarments and shoes.

The tailor found a dress suit and two sports jackets and slacks for Dan and also gave him shoes and all the other items he would need for his stay in New York. Dan stopped the tailor and seamstress as they left the suite and asked them how much he owed them for the clothing. The tailor replied, "The clothing is compliments of the president of the Museum of Modern Art, Nelson Rockefeller. He was very pleased to get back the museum's stolen paintings."

As the door closed, Kate said, "Nelson Rockefeller is buying us clothes?"

Dan and Kate then talked about all the priceless art they had seen in Bailey's collection and remembered three paintings that had been stolen from the Museum of Modern Art. "Bailey had an amazing collection." Dan said. "I am starving, Kate. Let's order a late lunch and take advantage of our dining room."

Dan called room service and ordered lunch. Fifteen minutes later, room service rang the doorbell at the dining room entrance and placed a linen tablecloth and two table settings on the long table. The waiter then moved a cart into the dining room and placed the food on the table, complete with a bottle of champagne. He also left a large envelope that contained an invitation to the Empire Room that night for dinner and a performance by Louis Armstrong.

Dan brought Kate to the dining room, pulled out her chair, and adjusted it for her as she sat down. Kate laughed, "You are such a gentleman. Well, at least Marilyn Monroe thought so."

Dan poured the champagne and raised his glass. "To my wonderful fiancée."

The telephone rang as they finished their lunch. Dan answered the phone and talked to Sperry, who told him a team of FBI agents watching a New York City mob boss saw Veronica Bailey go into the gangster's headquarters. They then followed her when two men drove her to the New York City pier, where the Italian ocean liner *Cristoforo Columbo* was boarding.

The agents tried to follow Bailey onto the ship but were stopped by an officer at the gangway. The Italian Line representative met with them and told the agents that Veronica Bailey's name was not on the passenger list, and that nobody meeting her description was onboard the ship. The ship sailed for Genoa before the agents could get clearance to search the ship. Sperry told Dan it was obvious that Bailey had very close ties to the mafia and would continue to be a serious threat to them.

Sperry told them that he would pick them up at eleven in the morning to bring them to City Hall, where the mayor had arranged a press conference to publicly thank them for helping to recover the priceless stolen art. He also warned them to stay inside the Waldorf Towers, where O'Brian and his men could protect them from Bailey's hit men.

Dan asked Sperry how long they needed to stay in New York City and was told that he could go ahead and make plans to leave the following day.

Dan finished the phone call, then walked to where Kate was sitting and handed her gun back, saying, "Sperry told me that Bailey has definite ties to the mob, and we will need to be extremely careful. I would feel much better if you had this for protection."

Dan then called and left a message with the hotel desk that he would like to talk to Mr. O'Brian. A few minutes later, the doorbell rang, and O'Brian was at the door. Dan invited the big Irishman into the living room area, and O'Brian told him that Sperry had filled him in on what had happened and the danger they were in. Dan told him that he wanted to get a gun for himself and some ammunition for Kate's gun. O'Brian told Dan he could arrange for him to get a gun and ammunition from a gun shop a couple of blocks from the hotel in the morning. Dan would have to check with O'Brian at about eight in the morning, so he could arrange an escort to the gun shop by a New York City police officer. O'Brian walked over to Kate, examined her gun, and said, "I can see this charming Irish lass can take of herself."

Kate walked with him to the doorway and thanked him for watching over them during their stay at hotel. He smiled at her as he left and told Dan, "You better take good care of Kate."

Dan called the concierge and asked him to book a bedroom compartment for him and Katherine Kelly on the next day's *Broadway Limited* connecting to the *California Zephyr* in Chicago with a final destination of Sacramento. Dan and Kate relaxed for a few hours and then got ready for dinner. The concierge called Dan and told him that he had reserved two bedroom compartments on the *California Zephyr* through-car on the *Broadway Limited* for them, and he would have their tickets delivered to their room.

"Kate, I am certainly going to leave the concierge a very large tip. He managed to do the impossible."

Dan explained that the Pennsylvania Railroad's *Broadway Limited* had a dedicated *California Zephyr* railroad car that allowed passengers to travel all the way to California without changing cars in Chicago. He had tried to book a bedroom on that car many times and had been unsuccessful. The concierge had managed to get two bedrooms on the car on short notice.

Dan and Kate took the tower elevator to the hotel lobby, then walked to the Waldorf's Empire Room. Dan gave the maître d' their invitation, and he seated them at a table for two right off the stage. A photographer immediately came to their table and took their photograph.

The Empire room was the perfect place for the concert. The large rectangular room was arranged with tables surrounding the orchestra stage. The twenty-foot-tall walls were trimmed in blue and gold, with large French crystal chandeliers and soaring arched windows overlooking Park Avenue.

Their waiter came to their table right after they were seated and took their dinner order. Kate ordered Lobster Newberg and a Waldorf salad, and Dan chose Veal Oscar, a green salad with Thousand Island dressing, and red velvet cake for dessert.

The wine steward came to their table with a towel-wrapped, chilled bottle of champagne. He placed two tall champagne flutes on their table, then showed Dan the bottle label. Dan nodded in approval, and the steward carefully opened the bottle and poured the sparkling wine into their glasses. He then placed a cork in the bottle and placed it in the chiller stand beside the table.

Dan raised his glass toward Kate and said, "To my beautiful fiancée and partner in life."

"Thank you, Dan."

They enjoyed a few sips of the champagne before the waiter arrived and served dinner. Kate saved her Waldorf salad for dessert, but when she tried a bite of Dan's cake, she asked the waiter to bring her own slice of the cake. The waiter cleared the table at showtime and poured more champagne in their glasses as the orchestra started to play. Louis Armstrong took the center of the stage and played several of his favorite songs. Later in the show, he left the stage and came to their table, and after escorting Kate to the stage, he sang to her. He then brought Kate back to her table and returned to the stage to perform his closing number.

Kate was on cloud nine the rest of the evening. They stopped for a late-night drink at a lounge off Peacock Alley, then returned to their room.

TRACK 61 ELEVATOR AT THE WALDORF

Photo by Joseph Brennan (Abandoned Stations)

CHAPTER SIXTEEN

Track 61
Escape

They had breakfast in their dining room early the next morning, so that Dan could meet with O'Brian. Kate opened the *New York Times* that had been delivered with breakfast and said, "Take a look at the front-page headlines and picture in the *Times*! The headline says *World's Largest Recovery of Stolen Art Here in New York City,* and there is a photograph of us in the Empire Room."

Dan and Kate read the article, which said that archeologists Dr. Daniel Strong and Dr. Katherine S. Kelly had climbed out of the seventy-seventh floor of the Chrysler building to escape from art thieves and then helped the FBI recover the world's largest collection of stolen art. The FBI recovered over fifty priceless works of art that had been stolen from museums around the world. Special Agent John Sperry of the FBI stated that there was no way to place an exact value on the stolen treasure, as most of the art was priceless and considered national treasures. Kate said, "Wow, a front-page picture in the *New York Times*. We better get a couple extra copies to show the crew back in California."

Dan then went down to the lobby and met with O'Brian, who introduced him to a pair of New York City police officers he had asked to escort Dan to the gun shop. Dan and the officers exited onto 50th Street and were walking the few blocks to the shop when a yellow cab hit a pedestrian crossing the street in front of them. One of the policeman told Dan to go ahead into the shop, while both policemen went to help the injured pedestrian.

Dan entered the gun shop, and the gunsmith brought him down to a basement pistol range. He then placed a Colt .38 Detective Special on the counter and loaded the gun with six bullets. He handed the gun to Dan and told him to see how he liked it. Dan raised the gun and shot three times at the range target. He saw a tight cluster of three shots just to the left of the X. He then shot three more times and the cluster neatly cut out the X in the center of the target. Dan said, "This is a great pistol."

The gunsmith replied, "Nothing but the best for a friend of Sergeant O'Brian."

The gunsmith quickly cleaned the revolver and asked Dan if he wanted it loaded. Dan said he did, and the gunsmith reloaded the gun and fitted Dan's shoulder holster. He gave Dan a gun-cleaning kit and a box of ammunition for his gun and Kate's gun. Dan signed all the paperwork and paid the gunsmith before returning to 50th Street.

Dan looked around the street when he came out of the shop but could not see the policemen who had escorted him to the shop, so he decided to walk the two blocks back to the Waldorf without them. He had walked less than a block when he noticed two men walking through the street traffic in his direction. When he reached the corner of the Waldorf, he saw a man in a dark suit at the Waldorf Tower entrance look at him and start walking his way.

Dan heard a gunshot, and the bullet hit the granite building bedside him. He turned and saw the two men across the street both had their guns drawn and were firing at him. He ducked into the Waldorf garage entrance and took cover behind a car. The three men entered the garage and split up to search for Dan. Dan shot one of the men who was walking straight at him and then ran toward the hotel entrance. The two remaining men started firing at him, shattering car windshields on both sides of him.

Dan could tell he would not be able to reach the hotel lobby and remembered the elevator that Sperry had described that went to the railroad track below the Waldorf.

Dan ran out the 49th Street garage exit and found the polished brass freight elevator door, but could not find a way to open it. He then saw a brass fire escape doorway immediately beside the elevator door, shot the lock, and opened the door. He could see a long staircase descending to the railroad siding below. He slammed the door and started down the staircase. The staircase door opened when he was halfway down the stairs and he shot at the two men in the doorway. The men returned fire just as he reached the railroad platform at Track 61.

He looked at the platform and saw the freight elevator that had been used to bring FDR's car to the railroad siding. Looking around, he could see that the Waldorf Astoria had been built over a network of railroad tracks, leading from Grand Central

Terminal. The tracks under the hotel appeared to be storage tracks on the Lexington Avenue side, but he could also see dozens of active tracks under Park Avenue, with trains arriving and departing from the station.

Dan jumped from the platform to the track level and shot at the two gunmen as they tried to leave the staircase. One of the men managed to take cover behind a support post on the platform and fired at him. Dan then ran alongside an active track headed toward the station. He crossed over two more tracks and was almost hit by a train arriving at the station. The two gunmen tried to follow but were blocked by train traffic.

Dan managed jump up to a handrail at the end of one of the passenger cars and placed a foot into a stirrup and rode the train until it stopped. He then ran along the train platform until he reached Grand Central Terminal and entered the building on the Track #34 platform. Inside the station, he found a policeman and explained that two gunmen were shooting at him, and he needed to contact FBI Agent Sperry as soon as possible.

The guard brought Dan to the station's security office, and Sperry arrived about fifteen minutes later. "Dan, I thought I told you to stay in your room at the Waldorf."

Sperry took Dan back to the Waldorf and left him with O'Brian in the hotel lobby. As he left, Sperry told Dan he would be back at ten to take them to City Hall. O'Brian looked at Dan and said, "I suppose you are responsible for all the shooting and broken windshields in my parking garage? I have not had this much excitement at the hotel since Marilyn Monroe got off the Towers elevator and decided to walk through the lobby in her bathrobe."

O'Brian escorted Dan back to the forty-second floor penthouse. When he reached the suite, O'Brian told Kate she needed to keep Dan out of trouble. She looked at Dan and said, "What happened this time?"

O'Brian told her that Dan had just shot up his parking garage during a running gun battle with mob hit men that ended at Grand Central Terminal. "Two of the gunmen got away, but the police hauled off one gunman that Dan had managed to shoot in my garage," O'Brian said. He then smiled and told Dan he was glad that he was safe, but next time he better follow directions, and wait for the police escort.

O'Brian left the suite, and Kate told Dan he was a trouble magnet, attracting trouble everywhere he went. "No, Kate, Bailey is providing all the trouble she can and will not give up until she gets her revenge."

Kate and Dan got ready to meet the mayor and packed their bags so that they would be ready for the train. At ten they took their bags and went down the elevator to the Waldorf Tower entrance. O'Brian was waiting for them at the elevator door. Kate walked up to him, gave him a big hug, and thanked him for looking out for them during their stay. He walked them out to Sperry's car, which was waiting at the curb.

Sperry then drove them to lower Manhattan and parked in City Hall Park. They walked to the front steps of City Hall, where there was a crowd waiting for the mayor's press conference. Sperry introduced them to the head of police security and he escorted them to up the steps and into the building to the Blue Room where the mayor would hold the press conference. The mayor's assistant then brought Dan and Kate to the podium and introduced them to the mayor.

The press conference started a few minutes later. The mayor stood at the podium and introduced Dr. Daniel Strong and Dr. Katherine S. Kelly to the press. He told the assembled correspondents that the two archeologists from California had actually climbed out of the top floor of the Chrysler building to escape from a group of art thieves and then assisted the FBI in the recovery of the world's largest collection of stolen art, which included a priceless collection of paintings stolen from New York City's Museum of Modern Art.

The mayor then said, "We have a tradition here in New York City of bestowing a key to the city to distinguished persons and honored guests."

Calling Dan and Kate real American heroes, he gave each of them a small wooden box with a gold key to the city. After the presentation, the mayor walked with Kate and Dan to his office, where he personally thanked them.

PENNSYLVANIA STATION

Photo by U. S. Library of Congress

CHAPTER SEVENTEEN

The Broadway Limited

Sperry was waiting for them when they left the mayor's office. He walked with them back to his car and told them it was time to head to Penn Station to catch their train. Dan told Sperry he could see a police car was following them. Sperry told them that the mayor wanted to make certain that there were no more attacks on the two of them in New York City.

Sperry drove past of a colonnade of pink granite Doric columns and stopped at the monumental entrance to Pennsylvania Station. Kate said, "This is an archeologist's dream building. Look, the entrance looks like the Brandenburg Gate."

Sperry parked the car, and they entered the station's colossal Travertine walled waiting room. Kate looked around and said, "This room was inspired by the Roman Baths of Caracalla and is as big as the St. Peter's Basilica's naïve in the Vatican."

"Yes, Kate, this the largest inside building space in New York City," said Sperry.

They then walked into a huge, arched, framed wall of glass and steel that formed the station's concourse. They walked through the concourse and into the glass-framed train shed and descended a staircase to the track platform. The fourteen-car Tuscan Red train was on the track in front of them. Kate noticed that the next-to-last car was gleaming stainless steel and did not match the rest of the train.

"How come that one is silver?" she asked.

Dan answered, "That is the *California Zephyr* through-sleeper we will be taking all the way to Sacramento."

They walked to the sleeping car and saw "CALIFORNIA ZEPHYR" in bold black letters and a smaller sign at eye level that said "SILVER RAPIDS." They gave their bags to the Pullman porter and entered the car through the vestibule with car number "CZ 11." Sperry walked with them through a narrow passageway lined with five roomettes on each side until they arrived at Kate's bedroom compartment. Dan walked to the next bedroom compartment, went to the center of the room, and opened a door that led into to Kate's adjoining room. He entered Kate's room and said, "I will have the porter open the wall in the morning, so we can have one large room during the daytime."

Sperry came into the room and told them they would have an FBI agent in the closest roomette to Kate's bedroom during the entire trip to California. He told them to try to avoid contact with him so no one would suspect he was watching them. "We will also have an agent meet you in Chicago to help you during your layover there," he told them. "I have to leave now, but I want to thank you both for all of your help recovering Bailey's stolen art. Have a safe trip to California."

Sperry then left the sleeping car and watched the entrance from the station platform until the train departed Penn Station.

The Pullman porter came to Kate's door and welcomed them aboard the *Broadway Limited*. He asked them if they would like to make a diner reservation. "Seven o'clock would work fine for us," Dan replied.

The porter then explained the features of their rooms and asked if they would like him to open the room divider in the morning. Dan said, "That would be great. By the way, what is your name?"

The porter answered, "Most people just call me George."

Kate asked, "What is your given name?"

"My name is Samuel, ma'am. But my friends call me Sam."

"Sam it will be. We hope to be your friends," Kate said with a smile.

"Thank you, ma'am."

Dan told Sam they would be going back to the observation car to have a drink before dinner. They walked toward the rear of the train as soon as Sam left the room. They passed four more bedroom compartments, opened two doors between cars, and entered the "Mountain View" observation car. They made their way to the back of the car and sat at a table in the observation lounge.

Dan told Kate that by taking the seven o'clock seating, they would avoid the rush on the diner that would occur when the train reached Philadelphia. The lounge attendant came to their table; Kate ordered a dry martini, and Dan ordered a Cuba Libre. After they ordered, a man in a dark blue suit entered lounge and gave a slight nod toward them as he sat alone at a table across the lounge.

"That must be our babysitter, Dan."

Dan and Kate watched the New Jersey landscape passing by out of the rear windows of the car as they sped toward their next station stop in Philadelphia. Dan told Kate that they would have to be careful whenever the train made a station stop. He explained that anyone gunning for them would make their move during the confusion of the loading and unloading of passengers. They would strike quickly and get off the train as quickly as possible. They would not want to be stuck on the train after a shooting.

"Wonderful. Now I am not going to sleep a wink tonight," said Kate.

They finished their drinks and left the observation car about fifteen minutes before the station stop in Philadelphia. They walked forward through the train, past their sleeping car and four more sleeping cars, before reaching the dining car. A dining car steward named Kresyl greeted them, and a waiter named Carter promptly took their dinner order. Dan ordered a broiled sirloin steak, and Kate ordered roast prime rib.

They both looked around the diner as the train stopped in Philadelphia, but the few diners in the car did not look like a threat. The man in the dark blue suit entered the diner and was seated near the entrance to the car with a good view of all the patrons in the dining car.

They had a leisurely dinner, noticing that there was a rush on the dining car about a half hour after they left Philadelphia. They finished their coffee and dessert and walked back to their sleeper and discovered the porter had made up their beds.

Dan checked Kate's room and gave her a kiss before he went through the door to his bedroom. Kate locked the bedroom door to the corridor and opened the door between their two bedrooms before she went to bed.

Dan and Kate both got up early the next morning, and Sam set up a table in Kate's bedroom. The room service waiter brought breakfast to the room from the diner. Dan tipped him for making the long trip with the heavy breakfast tray.

As they finished their breakfast, they noticed that there was some sort of commotion in the passageway. Sam said, "The gentleman in the next roomette is unconscious on the floor, and it looks like he was attacked. He must be a policeman, because his badge was lying on the floor beside him."

"The man was on the train to protect Kate and me," Dan told him.

Sam told them he had already contacted the conductor, and he was on the way from the front of the train. "Let me get you two to a safe place until the conductor gets here."

Sam brought them back to the observation lounge car and locked the door to the car from the outside so that no one from the front of the train could enter the last car. Dan looked outside the railroad car and could see that the train was about to enter Chicago Union Station. Just before they entered the station's train shed, he saw a man jump from the moving train and roll on the ground.

Sam returned with the conductor a few minutes later and opened the door to the lounge car. The conductor told them that a man had just jumped from the train, and they suspected he was responsible for attacking the FBI agent that was on their sleeping car. The conductor said the FBI and railroad police were waiting to board the train as soon as it reached the station platform.

Dan and Kate returned to their sleeping car and saw that the FBI agent was already receiving medical attention from a physician that was on the train. The agent was conscious and told the conductor he had been struck in the head, as he left his roomette to check Dr. Kelly's bedroom compartment. Sam told the conductor, "I saw a man leave the roomette and head toward the rear of the train, but he stopped when he saw me standing in the corridor outside this lady's bedroom. He turned around and ran toward the front of the train."

The conductor told them he had seen a man jump from the vestibule of the car, just before the train entered the station. He was most likely the same man who mugged the FBI agent.

CHICAGO UNDERGROUND RAILROAD

CHAPTER EIGHTEEN

Chicago Underworld

The train stopped at the station platform, and the sleeping car immediately filled with FBI agents and railroad police. They checked on the injured FBI agent, and then the conductor gave a report of events to the lead FBI agent. Dan recognized the lead agent. It was Charles Chambers, whom he had briefly met when he landed in Denver.

Chambers finished questioning the conductor and Sam, then looked at Dan and said, "I hear a lot has happened since I met you a few days ago, Dr. Strong. I heard you managed to rescue your partner from the art thieves."

Chambers told him that he had received reports from Jim Sperry in New York City and from Jack Packard in California, and he was aware of everything that had happened, including the recovery of the stolen art and Veronica Bailey's attempts to eliminate the two of them.

He told Dan and Kate that he and his men would be responsible for protecting them during their layover in Chicago and during the rest of their train trip back to California. Chambers told them that he wished he could tell them that Elliott Ness and the Untouchables had eliminated the Chicago mob, but it was still alive and a major problem in Chicago. "We know that Bailey has a contract out to eliminate you two, and there is no shortage of mob hit men in the Windy City," he warned them. "Stay close to my men, and be alert at all times."

Dan and Kate followed Chambers out of the sleeping car and onto the station platform. Chambers led the way, accompanied by an escort of four FBI agents. As they walked down the platform, Dan explained to Kate, "Chicago's Union Station has a very unusual layout. Trains do not run through the station—they begin or end their trips here. All passengers traveling through Chicago have to change trains in the station. There are twenty-four tracks coming from the north and twenty-four tracks coming from the south, and the north and south track platforms are connected by a concourse. Odd-numbered platforms are on the north side, and even-numbered platforms are on the south side. If your destination is Chicago, you walk through the concourse to the Grand Hall, and you can exit the station on Canal Street."

Chambers led the way as they passed through the concourse and entered the Grand Hall. Kate was impressed with the huge hall, with its American Renaissance Period architecture, vaulted skylight, marble floor, and Corinthian columns.

They walked toward the staircase to Canal Street, and suddenly the sound of gunshots echoed through the hall. Dan and Kate dropped to the marble floor and hid behind a bench as the FBI agents pursued the gunmen. Dan pulled out his gun and shielded Kate with his body. Out of the corner of his eye, Dan saw two gunmen walking toward them with their guns pointing at him.

Dan fired. The bullet struck one man in the leg, and he went down. Dan and Kate then ran back to the station's concourse and onto a train platform. They ran beside the dark green-and-orange cars of the *Empire Builder* and saw two men running after them. They soon reached a railway post office car near the front end of the train. The postal clerks were busy loading last-minute bags of mail onto the car when one of the gunmen opened fire on them. Dan said, "That was a big mistake. No one interferes with the United States Mail."

The railway postal clerks were armed, and they returned fire on the gunman. Dan and Kate hid behind a mail cart as the gunman made a hasty retreat. During the commotion, the second gunman managed to walk past the postal car unnoticed.

Dan looked around the platform and noticed a freight elevator nearby. He and Kate ran to the elevator without the gunman noticing them. Dan opened the gate to the elevator, and they climbed in. He pushed the control handle down, and the elevator descended below the station platform. As the elevator moved downward, they could see the second gunman looking down at them from the station platform. The elevator stopped about forty feet below the platform, and they walked out into a cave-like area. There were several egg-shaped tunnels with narrow railroad tracks leading off in several directions. The tunnels were only about seven feet tall and six feet wide. Kate asked, "Is this some sort of mine?"

"No, Kate, I think we have just stumbled into the Chicago Tunnel Company Railroad."

Dan explained that the tracks connected to all the major streets in Chicago's Loop area and were used to deliver freight to all the major businesses in Chicago.

Suddenly the elevator started back up to the railroad platform above.

"Kate, we'd better get moving. Bailey's hired gun will be here soon."

They ran into one of the dark tunnels and discovered a small freight locomotive on the track in front of them. They climbed onto it and Dan looked at the controls.

"I hope they still have the electric power on."

The gunman started shooting at them as Dan fumbled with the controls. Kate pulled out her gun and shot at the gunman. Suddenly, the locomotive came to life, and the headlight came on, brightly illuminating the tunnel and temporarily blinding the gunman. Dan pushed a control lever, and the locomotive started moving toward the gunman. He quickly reversed the direction of the lever and the locomotive sped down the tunnel away from the gunshots of their pursuer. The locomotive left Bailey's man in the dark as it sped through the narrow tunnel.

After a couple of minutes, the locomotive came to an intersection with another tunnel, and the track switch was set to make the locomotive turn left into another tunnel. They traveled a short distance before they reached another intersection and turned right. Dan noticed several railroad sidings with loading docks as they traveled through this tunnel, and after a traveling straight through a couple of track intersections, he stopped at a siding that he could see had an open door off the loading dock. Kate and he then walked through the open door into a sub-basement warehouse area filled with cases and kegs of beer. He looked at the beer labels and said, "I think I know where we are."

Dan told Kate, "All the beer has the Berghoff label. We must be in the storeroom for the Berghoff Bar. I always make a stop here when I visit Chicago. The restaurant has fantastic German food, and the sandwiches are to die for."

They climbed the stairs to the next level, walked through another storage area, climbed another set of stairs to the ground floor, and walked out into the bar. They could see that the ornate wooden bar ran the entire length of the building and was packed elbow-to-elbow with workingmen and businessmen alike. As they walked on the checkerboard-tiled floor through the dark, wood-paneled bar section, Dan told Kate, "We'd better get through here quickly; the bar has a strict men-only policy." They reached a blue curtained doorway and walked through it into the Berghoff Restaurant. "You are safe here," Dan said. "Women are allowed in the restaurant."

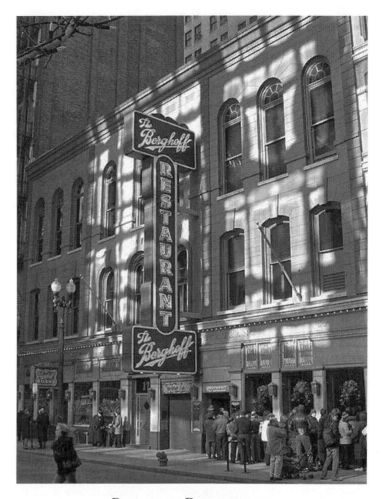

BERGHOFF RESTAURANT

Photo by David K. Staub

A waiter promptly seated them at a table in the corner of the room, and Dan went to the telephone, called the FBI office, and asked for agent Chambers. Chambers was surprised to hear from him; he was afraid Bailey's men had managed to capture them. Dan told him that they were at the Berghoff Restaurant on Adams Street. Dan then laughed and asked,

"Would you like me to order some sandwiches for you and your men?"

"Sure! Order four corned beef on rye sandwiches, and I will be there in ten minutes."

Dan returned to Kate's table and told her that Chambers was on the way to meet them. The waiter came to take their order. Kate ordered a cheeseburger, and Dan ordered five corned beef on rye sandwiches.

"My God, Dan, are you really that hungry?" Kate asked in amazement.

Dan laughed and told her, "Chambers" men are very hungry after this morning's excitement at Union Station, and they will be joining us for lunch."

Kate looked around the large dining room and noticed the oak paneling and columns. The brown-and-cream-colored linoleum tiled floor was scattered with low-slung wooden tables with white linen tablecloths, and brass chandeliers hung from the twenty-foot ceiling. She looked toward the street entrance and saw that Chambers and three of his agents had arrived. Chambers sat down with them, and the three agents sat at the next table. Chambers said, "You two gave us a good scare this morning. I knew that Bailey was serious about eliminating you two, but I never dreamed they would attack FBI agents in the middle of the Grand Hall at Union Station."

Chambers asked them how they had managed to escape, and Dan told him that they managed to get into the Chicago Tunnel Railroad and escaped from the gunmen in the tunnels below Chicago.

"You two are lucky you got out of the tunnels. You can get lost for days in that dark tunnel system."

During lunch Chambers told Dan and Kate that the director had approved placing two agents onboard the *California Zephyr* to escort them back to Sacramento. "I will be one of your escorts and will be in the roomette closest to Kate's bedroom. The other agent will be one car in front of us and will keep an eye on passengers headed to the back of the train. We have already checked out the sleeping car passengers riding between you and the observation car at the end of the train, so we should have a very secure area on the train without alarming the public. I am certain that Bailey knows we will be on the train, so it is not likely that she will do anything before you reach California."

THE CALIFORNIA ZEPHYR

Photo – R. Orlandella Collection

CHAPTER NINETEEN

Westbound on the California Zephyr

After lunch, Kate and Dan walked with Chambers to his car and drove back to Union Station. Chambers waited for his agents to surround Kate and Dan, and then they walked into the Great Hall and headed to the concourse. As they walked through the concourse, Kate said, "The glass vaulted concourse reminds me of the concourse at Penn Station in New York."

They then walked into the dark train shed and saw the *California Zephyr* waiting on the platform. The matched stainless steel cars glimmered, and the neon "CALIFORNIA ZEPHYR" drumhead at the end of the bullet-shaped tail car glowed a bright orange, with wisps of steam coming from under the car.

"Dan, this looks like something out a Buck Rogers movie," Kate said. As they walked along the side of the car, she noticed a glass-domed observation area on the top of the car. "What is that glass bubble for?"

Dan explained, "The California Zephyr is a very special train, designed to give its passengers spectacular daylight views of the Rockies and the Sierra. The glass bubble is called a 'vista dome,' and there are five cars on the train with vista domes. The car you are looking at has both a dome and an observation area at the end of the train. It is reserved for Pullman sleeper passengers only." As they walked along the car, they could see the name of the car was *Silver Crescent.* "The next car up is the Silver Rapids sleeper that we took from New York City."

Chambers's men entered the car, then quickly returned and told Chambers that the car was clear. He followed Kate and Dan to their bedroom compartments and said he would be in the next roomette if they needed anything.

Kate and Dan entered their bedrooms and saw that Sam had removed the partition between their rooms, so they had one large suite. Dan then told Kate more about the *California Zephyr.*

He told her that the layout of the train between their car and the diner was very similar to the *Broadway Limited,* but the cars in front of the diner were totally different. "The first car in front of the diner is a vista dome buffet lounge car for light snacks. In front of that car, you will find three vista dome coach cars. The diner actually serves as a dividing point between the passengers traveling by coach and the Pullman sleeping car passengers. The coach passengers are not supposed to travel past the diner to the rear of the train, but the sleeping car passengers can go anywhere on the train they wish."

Sam greeted them and said he hoped that their trip would be much quieter on the way to California. Dan thanked him for helping them earlier when the gunman was onboard the train. Sam smiled and left a silver pitcher of ice water in the room for them.

The train started to move out of the Union Station train shed and slowly picked up speed as it passed through the rail yard. A young uniformed woman, called a "Zephyrette," stopped at their bedroom and introduced herself to Dan and Kate. She said she was the train's hostess and would be narrating points of interest along the route. They should feel free to call her if there was anything they needed during the trip, she said. She then asked them if she could make a reservation for the diner. Dan told her that they would like to eat at six.

Dan and Kate then went back to the vista dome lounge for a drink. Dan looked down the aisle to and made eye contact with Chambers, who acknowledged the look with a nod of his head. They stopped at the curved lounge bar under the dome and ordered their drinks, then walked back to the Pullman lounge at the tail of the train. Before they could sit down in the lounge chairs, Kate said, "Let's take our drinks up the stairs to the vista dome seating area."

They went up the curved staircase, found a pair of seats at the front of the dome, and watched the Illinois countryside pass them by. Dan told Kate, "Wait until we are in the Rockies tomorrow. Then you will see some amazing scenery."

They stayed in dome for about an hour and then returned to their room. They sat down near the window, and Dan said,

"Now that we are heading home, it is time to focus on our work in California. First, we have to summarize what has already been accomplished, and then we need to determine our next steps at Alta and at Donner Pass."

Kate told Dan that the project was very successful in Murphys. The students had done an excellent archeological survey of the town and verified the location of the buildings and the cavern mentioned in Doc Strong's Journal. Richardson's notebook provided a separate written account that validated the entries in Doc Strong's journal. Dan told Kate, "Now we must plan the hard part of the project—validating the existence of Judah's gold and finding its hiding place. We have collected a great deal of information that has given us clues to find the gold. There is very little left at Alta of archeological value. It was all washed away by years of hydraulic mining in the area. We need to analyze the clues we have found during the project and see if we can solve our puzzle." Dan and Kate then made a list of the clues for the gold's hiding place.

Doc Strong's Journal
Tells about Judah's gold in general terms

The Fifty-Dollar Gold Coin
Validates the existence of the gold

Judah's Purchase Option
Proves Judah was paid $100,000

Wells Fargo Receipt
Proves Doc Strong received $100,000 in gold coin

Jim Smiley's Watch
Contains several clues to the gold's location

Cigar Box—Missing Page
Points to Donner Pass location + Number 1053

Richardson's Notebook
Points to Donner Pass location and Clamper Gold in Murphys

Jones Pharmacy Book
Proves Clamper $300,000 investment

Judah's Plumb Bob
Key for hiding place of Judah's gold

Spike numbered 1053
Key for hiding place of Judah's gold.

"Kate, the information we have points to Donner Pass as the hiding place for Judah's gold, and I believe your watch is the key to finding the gold's exact location at Donner Pass."

The outside of the watch said: **Jim Smiley, Supreme Noble Humbug, Murphy's Diggins.**

The edge of the watch had the points of the compass, with an arrow pointing east.

N

W   E->

S

The engraving on the inside of the watchcase said: **ECV Stake Is Found where the Sacramento Crossed CPRR.**

Dan told Kate that he believed the inscription was the real clue to the gold's location, and if they could decipher its meaning, they would know the exact location of Judah's gold.

"There is no use looking for the gold's hiding place until we find a way to do away with Bailey's constant attempts to kill us," hc said. "As long as she believes that she can find Judah's gold without our help, she will try to eliminate us. We have to find a way to convince her that we know the exact location of the gold, and the easiest way for her get to the gold is to follow us. She would call off her hit men and have Damian keep track of us. Bailey has a huge ego and will want to be present when the gold's hiding place is discovered."

"Somehow we need to set a trap for her," Kate said. "That is the only way we can return to our normal lives."

Kate and Dan walked forward to the dining car and ate dinner. They stopped at Chambers's room on the way back and asked him to go back to the observation car with them. They went together to the end of the observation car and sat down in the lounge chairs. Dan told Chambers they needed to find a way to get Bailey to call off her gang of hit men. He explained, "If we convince Bailey that we know the exact location of the hidden gold, she will call off the gunmen, so she can follow us to the gold. Bailey will most likely have Bradford Damian follow us, but she will want to see the gold discovery in person. We need to set a trap to catch Bailey using Judah's gold as the bait."

"Dan, do you know where the gold is hidden?" Chambers asked.

"We know the gold is hidden somewhere near Donner Pass, but we do not know the exact location, because we have not deciphered all the information left to us by Doc Strong and Jim Smiley. Bailey knows Kate and I have the information that can lead us to the exact location of the gold. If we make her believe we have solved the puzzle, she will want us to do all the work of finding the gold's hiding place, and then she will try to take it away from us."

Dan then wrote a note to Packard, asking him to tell the archeology students in California that Kate and Dan had determined the location of Judah's gold, and that they wanted to meet with the entire project team at the Donner Ski Ranch near Donner Pass in four days. He told Packard to make certain that this information was leaked to Damian. Dan gave the note and money to the Zephyrette stewardess and asked her have it sent by Western Union telegram when they reached Denver.

Chambers informed Dan that Packard and his men would be picking them up in Sacramento.

Kate and Dan said goodnight to Chambers and walked to their rooms. Dan opened Kate's door and entered her room to check it. He could see the porter had made up her bed, and the door was open between their two compartments. He looked into his room and saw that it was safe as well. Kate entered the room and said, "Why don't you stay with me tonight?"

CHAPTER TWENTY

The Scenic Rockies

Dan and Kate had breakfast brought to their room early the next morning. They walked back to the vista dome observation car after the train stopped at Denver and found seats at the front of the observation area.

They watched as the train climbed the front range of the Rocky Mountains. As they traveled west, the train passed through about thirty tunnels, including the six-mile-long Moffat Tunnel under the Continental Divide. They stayed in the dome, watching spectacular views of the Rockies, until lunchtime, when they went to the dining car.

During lunch, they saw their train pass the eastbound *California Zephyr* at Glenwood Springs, Colorado. After lunch they went straight back to the vista dome in the observation car and watched the scenery until they passed through Ruby Canyon.

Kate said, "I can't believe we actually have had a day to enjoy our trip, free from attacks by Bailey and her men."

"Don't get too relaxed, Kate. Bailey has a nasty habit of surfacing when you least expect it."

Dan told Kate that it was time to plan the details of their trap for Bailey. "When we reach the Donner Ski Ranch, we will tell our team that Judah's gold is hidden in the lower China Wall between summit tunnels 7 and 8. It will be tricky getting to the wall, because it is directly under Southern Pacific Railroad's busy westbound mainline track."

Dan explained that the China Wall was a seventy-five-foot-tall retaining wall, composed of thousands of granite stones, to support the tracks of the railroad over a deep ravine between Tunnel 7 and Tunnel 8. The Chinese workers of the Central Pacific Railroad had built the impressive wall without mortar—it was held together entirely by gravity.

"We will have to coordinate our activity with Southern Pacific's maintenance-of-way crews in that area," Dan said. "The lower China Wall is isolated and would be the perfect place to catch Bailey. I just need a plan to get her take the bait and follow us there."

Dan and Kate then walked up to the dining car, and both ordered the Italian dinner special, which featured veal scaloppini. They returned to the observation car for an after-dinner drink and to work on the details of their plan to catch Veronica Bailey.

The train made a late-night stop in Salt Lake City, and as they pulled out of the station, Chambers ran into the lounge car and warned them that one of Bailey's men had just boarded the train. He told them to stay in their seats until his partner could locate the man on the train.

Dan and Kate instantly recognized Damian as he entered the lounge car. They told Chambers that Bradford Damian was a black-market archeologist hired by Bailey to follow them. Damian walked straight to Dan and Kate and said, "Just the couple I was looking for! I hope you have had a pleasant trip."

Dan glared at Damian and said, "What are you doing here, Damian? I told you to stay away from us."

Damian smiled and said he would like to talk to Dan about a business proposition.

"What does Bailey want now?" Dan asked.

Damian explained that his business proposal had nothing to do with Veronica Bailey. He would like to make an offer as an independent archeologist, wishing to assist them in finding Judah's gold.

"That is pure bullshit, Damian."

"Let's go down to the bar," Damian persisted. "I have a few things I would like to discuss with you."

Dan left Kate with Chambers and went down the steps to the tavern area with Damian. They sat a small table near the circular bar, and Dan said, "Okay, now you can tell me what you really want."

Damian said he knew that Kate and Dan had determined the exact location of Judah's gold. He explained that it was only a matter of time before Bailey's hired guns would be successful and kill Dan and Kate. Damian said he did not want to see them killed and claimed he could call off the gunmen, if Dan agreed to work with him. "Veronica Bailey's offer to split the gold evenly still stands," he added.

Dan told Damian, "I am aware that even though FBI agents surround us, it is only a matter of time before Bailey's persistence will break through our protective shield. I am interested in coming to an agreement. I would have to keep it secret, so that Kate and the FBI agents do not figure out that I am working with you.

"Protecting Kate is extremely important to me, and I do not trust Bailey. There is nothing to guarantee that she will not take all the gold and then kill us anyway. I will only agree to work with you if Veronica Bailey is present when we expose the gold's hiding place."

"I believe that can be arranged," Damian replied.

Dan then told Damian they would have to make it look like they kidnapped him when he got off the train in Sacramento. "It will not be easy, he warned, "because the FBI agents are protecting us." He told Damian that the best time to snatch him would be after the FBI agents on the train handed them off to Jack Packard in Sacramento.

He reminded Damian that he would not cooperate with them if any harm came to Kate.

Damian grinned and said, "We have a deal. Do not change your mind, or the results will be catastrophic for both of you."

Dan then returned to the rear of the train and sat down with Kate and Chambers. "What did he say?" Kate asked.

"Just as I expected, he offered to call off the hired guns if I agreed to work with Bailey," Dan replied.

Chambers got up from his seat and told them that he was going to keep an eye on Damian. Dan and Kate stayed in the lounge for a few minutes, then walked to their room and went to bed.

Dan and Kate went to breakfast in the diner early in the morning. The train stopped at Portola, and they watched Damian sprint to a pay phone at the train station and make a short telephone call. He hung up the phone and ran back to the train, just as the train conductor signaled the engineer to start the train.

"I bet he just called Bailey to fill her in on my agreement."

Dan and Kate walked back to the vista dome observation car, took their usual seats in the front of the dome, and watched the scenery in the Feather River Canyon. They went back to their room as they reached Oroville. Dan walked down the aisle to Chambers's roomette and talked to him for a few minutes, then returned to his room. Dan and Kate picked up their bags and headed to the vestibule of the sleeping car. Dan told Kate, "The stop in Sacramento is extremely short, because the train blocks the major streets in downtown Sacramento when it's at the depot."

Chambers and his partner joined them in the vestibule as the train pulled into Sacramento's mission-style Western Pacific depot. Dan and Kate went down the steps and walked toward the beige stucco arches of the depot across the "J" Street intersection.

DONNER SUMMIT TUNNELS

Photo by Ralph Orlandella (author)

CHAPTER TWENTY-ONE

Setting the Trap

Packard and his men met them as they got off the train. Chambers walked up to Packard and shook his hand; then, after a short conversation, he and his partner got back on the train.

Packard started walking toward the station with Kate at his side. Dan walked a few steps behind them. They crossed the street and entered the Spanish arched train platform, then walked toward the parking lot.

Suddenly, a car drove through their group and isolated Dan on the other side of the car. Packard made certain Kate was safely behind a car as he and his men tried to rush the car. The rear car door opened, and a man pointed a gun at Dan and ordered him to get in. The car's wheels smoked as the car sped out of the parking lot.

Packard and his men fired a few shots at the tires, but the car managed to speed away from the train station. Inside the car, one of the gunmen tied Dan's hand together and took Dan's gun out of his shoulder holster. They drove a short distance and stopped beside a black limousine in McKinley Park. Dan was told get out of the car and get into the limousine.

He entered the back door of the limousine and saw Veronica Bailey, sitting with one of her bodyguards. Dan sat in the seat facing her. He looked around the car and saw Damian sitting in the front passenger seat, giving directions to the driver. Dan noticed that the car with the two men who kidnapped him was following the limousine. Veronica Bailey smiled at Dan and said, "Well, Dr. Strong, you finally made the right decision. You and Dr. Kelly will no longer have to worry about dodging bullets. It is now time for you to show me the way to Judah's gold."

Bailey told her bodyguard to untie Dan's hands. She then asked for the two artifacts that would be used to unlock the gold's hiding place. Dan pulled out a Pullman berth key and a small cast metal table crumber he had gotten from their dining room waiter. Bailey put them in her purse without taking a good look at them.

Bailey told Dan that they were headed to Donner Pass, and she needed to know the exact location of Judah's gold. Dan paused for a second then said, "The gold coins are hidden in the China Wall between Tunnel 7 and Tunnel 8." Bailey asked Dan to give her more information about the China Wall. Dan told her, "There was a deep ravine between the two tunnels when they built the railroad, and the Chinese workers used thousands of granite stones to build a seventy-five-foot embankment to support the tracks between the two tunnels.

"There are two ways to get to the lower China Wall. The first is to come from above, either through the summit tunnel or from the granite top of Donner Pass. The second route is from below. You drive on Highway 40 and park near the rainbow bridge overlook, cross the road and walk through an area with stone petroglyph slabs, and then take a short hike to China Wall."

Dan warned them that approaching the site from above the China Wall would be dangerous, because they would have to cross a very active railroad right-of-way. Furthermore, the trains would arrive without warning, because the tunnels and snow sheds would hide them until the last minute.

"Okay, we will climb to the wall from below," said Bailey.

The limousine traveled along Highway 40, and as they passed through a roadway tunnel near Newcastle, Bailey said, "I know Packard and his men will be trying to follow us, so we will not be traveling to the China Wall today. We will travel to the north shore of Lake Tahoe and stay in cabins at the Cal Neva Lodge. My friends at the lodge will make certain no one knows we are there."

They drove past the Norden snow sheds and Soda Springs about an hour later. They then drove by Donner Ski Ranch, and past the road to Sugar Bowl Resort. After driving around a few curves, they crossed a large, arched concrete bridge. After crossing the bridge, Dan pointed out the China Wall on the mountainside above them.

The limousine continued driving past the bridge, and Dan looked back and noticed that Bailey's second car was no longer following the limousine. Bailey said, "My men slowed down to see if we are being followed."

They descended down a steep road grade to Donner Lake, drove beside the lake for a few miles, and turned right onto the road to Lake Tahoe's north shore.

They reached Lake Tahoe a half hour later, then drove along the lakeshore to the Cal Neva Lodge that was situated on top of the California-Nevada border. Bailey's limousine drove to the front door of the lodge, and Bailey, Dan, and one of her bodyguards entered the building. As they walked through the entry, Dan noticed a billboard sign with a picture of Frank Sinatra that said he would be performing in the showroom that evening.

Bailey looked at the sign and said, "Frank enjoys playing here so much that he and his partners are thinking of buying the place. You never know which celebrities will be here. In addition to the Rat Pack, I have seen many Hollywood celebrities enjoying themselves here, away from the prying eyes of their fans and the press."

Bailey met with the hotel manager, who told her that they had two bungalow cabins for her and that the staff had been told that she did not want anyone to know she was staying there.

The bellman then escorted them to a tunnel entrance under the lodge, which connected to several remote bungalows. As they walked through the tunnel, the bellman explained the tunnels were originally built during the prohibition and were used to smuggle liquor into the lodge from the lake. Later, they connected several of the bungalows so that people staying in the cabins would not have to walk through the winter snow to get to the main lodge. He told them that all the celebrity performers at the lodge now used the tunnel to maintain their privacy.

The bellman brought them up a staircase into Cabin 4, then escorted Dan and the guard outside to Cabin 3. The guard tipped the bellman, who quickly walked back to the lodge. The guard then brought Dan up a staircase to balcony overlooking the north shore of Lake Tahoe. He opened the door of the cabin and told him to stay inside.

Dan looked around the room and saw a telephone. He lifted the receiver and discovered the telephone line was dead. The interior of the cabin was very simple, with a bedroom, bathroom, and walk-in closet. He then looked out the window at the fabulous view of Crystal Bay and Lake Tahoe.

The guard opened the door to the cabin about an hour later and told Dan that he was going to have dinner with Bailey. He also told him not to try to escape or do anything stupid— there was nowhere to run. The guard brought him to the dining room, and Dan sat down with Bailey. Bailey had changed in to a stylish black and silver evening dress and was sitting with two middle-aged men dressed in expensive Italian tailored suits. She told Sam Giancana and Joseph Kennedy that Dan was a talented historian and archeologist who had agreed to show her the location of hidden treasure worth millions.

Sam asked if Frank would be joining them for dinner, and Bailey told them he was getting ready for his show and would see them later in the lounge.

Damian walked up to the table and told Bailey that the guards in the car that followed them had observed Packard and his agents turn off Highway 40 near Donner Ski Ranch, then drive to the university students' project site near the entrance of the summit tunnel. Bailey instructed Damian to take one of her men with him and return to the students' camp to keep an eye on Packard. Damian immediately headed to the door to drive back to Donner Pass.

Giancana asked Bailey, "Veronica, do you need any help with the Feds?"

"Thanks, Sam, but everything is under control and going as planned."

After dinner, Bailey, Giancana, and Kennedy walked to the showroom, and Sinatra greeted them as they entered the room. The guard left Dan in the "Indian Room" near a large stone fireplace and told him to stay put while he went to the restroom. A lounge waiter then asked Dan if he would like a drink, and Dan told him not yet. He asked the server, "Do you know much about the people I was with earlier?"

The waiter told him that all of them were regulars at the Cal Neva, and that he believed the two middle-aged men, Giancana and Kennedy, were investors in the lodge. He said Kennedy had been coming here since prohibition days and had been a supplier of bootleg liquor. Miss Bailey had started coming here a few years ago, the server went on, and appeared to be close a friend of Sinatra's. "She stays in Cabin 4, and Cabin 5 is always reserved for Sinatra. The two cabins are directly connected by an underground tunnel, and I am pretty sure she has made more than a few late-night visits to Sinatra's cabin. "She is also very close to Giancana, Al Capone's successor." The server then told Dan that he had said too much about Dan's dinner partners and walked away as the guard returned.

The guard asked Dan, "What was the bar server talking to you about?"

"He wanted to know if he could bring me a drink. Do you want me to call him back? I could sure use a cold beer about now."

The guard told Dan there would be no drinks for him that evening. He then walked with Dan back to Cabin 3 and told Dan, We will be watching this cabin all night, so do not leave it for any reason."

Dan turned off the lights inside the cabin and spent an hour enjoying the moonlit lake. Suddenly he saw a cabin cruiser arrive offshore without any lights. He started thinking it was strange to be cruising at night without any cabin lights, and then he noticed that the boat's red and green running lights were not on either. Someone must be watching the shore side cabins and the lodge. He thought that it would make no sense for Bailey's men to be watching and then concluded that it must be the FBI. He was confused, because Damian's gunmen had said that all of Packard's men were at Donner Pass.

Dan watched the boat for another hour, then went to bed. He woke up at sunrise and still saw the cabin cruiser anchored offshore. One of Bailey's men came into the cabin and escorted Dan to the lodge dining room. Bailey greeted Dan by saying, "Good morning, Dr. Strong. I hope you are ready for a very busy day."

They sat down in the dining room and ordered breakfast. Bailey told Dan they would be heading back to the China Wall that morning. Dan noticed that Bailey was dressed in hiking attire and appeared to be ready to do some climbing.

The waiter told Bailey she had a phone call, and she walked away for a few minutes. She returned and told Dan that Damian had reported that Packard and all his men believed that she would be going to Donner Pass to find the gold and had set a trap for her there. Bailey said, "It is time to make our move; we leave for China Wall in ten minutes."

"How do you plan to get the gold down to the road from China Wall?" Dan asked.

Bailey told Dan that she would not be taking the gold downhill, because she had arranged to have railroad speeder cars with trailers on the track above them. They would load the gold onto the rail cars and take them to Truckee.

"That's crazy! The Track 1 mainline is above Chinese Wall, and it is used for all westbound trains. A westbound train could sneak up on you out of a tunnel at any time, and there would be no way to escape."

Bailey told Dan she had arranged for a railroad mainte-nance-of-way worker to sabotage a the track just east of Truckee, which would stop all westbound trains in the Truckee River valley. "We will have several hours to get the gold down from the Chinese Wall before the track can be repaired and trains can head up the westbound track again. I will have enough men at China Wall to get the gold up to the waiting rail speeders in a matter of minutes."

Bailey told Dan it was time leave. They walked through the lobby and climbed into her limousine, followed by two of her men. Dan saw four additional men climb into the sedan that had followed them the day before. The two vehicles then drove along the lake and turned onto a road headed toward Truckee. They reached the outskirts of Truckee about a half hour later, then turned onto Highway 40 and drove along the length of the shore of Donner Lake. Near the end of the lake, they started a steep climb up the mountain and parked their cars at the Rainbow Bridge lookout.

Dan led Bailey and two of her men down the roadway to the opposite side of the road, where it was cluttered with large granite slabs. As they walked, they could see the engraved prehistoric petroglyphs on the slabs below their feet.

They continued climbing up the trail and came to the base of the China Wall. They looked up to the track above the wall and saw two railroad speeders come out of the Tunnel 7 snow shed and stop directly above them. Damian drove the first speeder, and one of his men drove the second.

Damian scrambled down the side of China Wall to meet them and said, "We have totally fooled Packard and his men. They are over near the ski lodge, waiting for you to arrive. They still think the gold is hidden at the top of Donner Pass."

Bailey pulled the two artifacts out her bag and said, "Dr. Strong, it is time to show me how these unlock the treasure vault."

As Dan started to take the artifacts, they heard gunfire echoing in the valley bellow and saw that several police cars surrounding the bridge overlook were in a gunfight with Bailey's men.

Bailey told Damian, "This is a trap! I knew Dr. Strong was too much of a boy scout, to help me steal the gold. We need to get out of here now!"

She and Damian and two of the gunmen then scrambled up to Track 1 over China Wall. Damian and Bailey climbed on to the first speeder and sped into Tunnel 8, just as Special

Agent Chambers and his men emerged from the tunnel behind them.

Bailey's two gunmen quickly realized they were surrounded and dropped their guns. Dan climbed the embankment, grabbed both guns, and said, "We can't let Bailey get away again."

Dan jumped into the second speeder, and Chambers jumped in with him. They raced after Bailey, but then Chambers looked at Dan and told him they had to turn back. "There is a westbound train headed right for us! The railroad switched the blocked westbound train to a parallel track so that it could reach Truckee. When it reached Truckee, they switched the train back to Track 1," he explained. "The train has already gone around Stanford's Curve and it is headed straight for us."

Dan continued to speed along the track and could see glimpses of Bailey ahead of them. They finally caught up to her in a tunnel. About that time, Dan saw a bright headlight moving toward them in the darkness of the tunnel.

Dan quickly reversed the direction of the speeder and started racing away from the oncoming train. He looked at Chambers and asked, "What type of train is heading toward us, freight train or passenger train?"

"Passenger train! I believe it was the City of San Francisco."

"Oh, crap! Why couldn't it be a slow moving freight train?"

Dan could see that Bailey and Damian had reversed the direction of their speeder as well, but the train was closing on them very quickly. Dan told Chambers, "Even if the train sees the speeder, it is unlikely that it could brake in time to prevent a collision. It would be suicide to jump when we are outside a tunnel or snow shed, because it is almost a straight drop to the valley below. We will we have to ride it until we emerge from the west portal of the summit tunnel."

Suddenly, they heard a train horn blast and a loud crashing sound echoing from behind them. Dan and Chambers saw the front of a locomotive collide with Bailey's speeder. The speeder derailed and was launched out of the tunnel portal into the valley below. Dan heard the sound of the train's brakes setting, but the locomotive continued to close the space between them. Dan and Chambers remained on the speeder and managed to stay a few feet ahead of the diesel locomotive. They entered the east portal of the summit tunnel with the train a few feet behind them. The locomotive finally started to slow down as they emerged from the west portal of the tunnel. They traveled out to the Summit valley and finally stopped near Norden, when the *City of San Francisco* stopped, inches behind them.

Chambers smiled at Dan and said, "Traveling by train with you is always an experience Dr. Strong."

"What in the world are you doing here, anyway, Charlie? I saw you get back on the train in Sacramento, and I was afraid you were heading home."

Chambers told him he was not about to let Bailey get away. He had climbed back on the train in Sacramento to convince Damian that he was he was no longer on the case. "We got off the train just before it left the station, and I coordinated my effort with Packard, just as we talked about on the train" he explained. "Just as you, Kate, and I discussed on the train, we knew that Damian would be watching Packard's every move, so we let him watch Packard set up a trap for Bailey at Donner Summit. I moved my men in when we were certain that Damian had taken the bait. I also had men high on a mountainside and in a cabin cruiser, keeping an eye on you at the Cal Neva Lodge. Kate tipped me off that you were going to tell Bailey that the gold was hidden in the China Wall, so was I able to set up my own trap for Bailey."

One of Chambers's men drove up, and they both got in the car and rode to the students' camp. Dan stepped out of the car and was tackled by Kate, who gave him a huge hug and said, "It's finally time to finish this project and find Judah's gold."

Dan just smiled, and they started walking to the campsite.

CHAPTER TWENTY-TWO

Solving the Puzzle

Kate and Dan walked through the student camp to their headquarters tent, and Dan said, "Kate, I believe I know where Judah gold is hidden."

Dan then explained the clues:

Doc Strong's Journal
Tells about Judah's gold in general terms

The Fifty-Dollar Gold Coin
Validates the existence of the gold

Judah's Purchase Option
Proves Judah was paid $100,000

Wells Fargo Receipt
Proves Strong received $100,000 in gold coin

Jim Smiley's Watch
Contains several clues to the gold's location

Cigar Box—Missing Page
Points to Donner Pass location + Number 1053

Richardson's Notebook
Points to Donner Pass location and Clamper gold

Jones Pharmacy Book
Proves Clamper $300,000 investment

Judah's Plumb Bob
Key for hiding place of Judah's gold

Spike numbered 1053
Key for hiding place of Judah's gold.

Dan told Kate he had figured out the hidden meaning on the engraving in Jim Smiley's gold pocket watch.

The engraving on the inside of the watchcase said: **ECV Stake Is Found where the Sacramento Crossed CPRR.**

Dan explained, "At first, the only thing I could think of was that Smiley was describing the Sacramento River waterfront, where the Central Pacific Railroad tracks met the Sacramento River. But this did not match any of the other clues that pointed to Donner Pass as the location of the gold. Then I remembered the number 1053 stamped on the head of the metal spike. At first I did not know the significance of the number, so I looked at the spike one more time and discovered the number actually was 105.3.

"I instantly knew that the number must be a milepost on the railroad, but the milepost for the Donner Summit is 195, and that was the closest point the railroad came to Donner Pass.

"Kate, I remembered a research report that you had written. You wrote the real location of the completion of the first transcontinental railroad was at a bridge just outside Lathrop, California. Before that time, the Central Pacific Railroad terminated at Sacramento. The completion of the bridge linked the railroad to the San Francisco bay area for the first time, and the railroad could truly run from coast to coast. Your report also stated that railroad changed their mileposts to measure the distance from San Francisco, instead of Sacramento." Dan smiled. "The original milepost for the Summit Tunnel was 105.17 when the railroad was built."

Dan then explained the significance of the number 105.3: "During the excavation of the summit tunnel, the Central Pacific Railroad's first assistant chief engineer, Lewis Clement, was in charge, and he decided that they should excavate a central shaft near the midpoint of the tunnel so that workers could excavate the tunnel from four headings. He must have used this metal spike to mark the location on top of the Summit Tunnel where the central shaft was to be excavated. If you were to measure to milepost 105.3 inside the tunnel, you would be standing directly under the central shaft.

"At first, I thought that Clement must have constructed a vault inside the tunnel at track level to hide the gold. But then I remembered the engraving inside Smiley's gold watch said the Clamper's stake is found where the Sacramento crossed the CPRR. "

"I was confused at first; then I remembered that when Clement dug the central shaft, he had a team of oxen drag a twelve-ton steam locomotive boiler to the top of the summit tunnel and used it to power a hoist to lift the excavated rock out of the central shaft.

"Kate, guess what the name of the steam locomotive was?"

"Oh, my God, it was the Sacramento!"

Dan then explained that Judah's gold and the miners' investment gold must be hidden inside the central shaft. "Lewis Clement knew the vault would be too accessible to railroad workers if it were hidden at track level inside the tunnel. He also knew that after the construction of the tunnel, there would never be a need for anyone to travel down the central shaft again. He had found the perfect hiding place for the gold." Dan smiled at Kate and said, "Let's go take a look."

Dan and Kate then met with the student team leaders and told them they needed to use one of the jeeps for about an hour. They also told them to have the students meet them at the central shaft on top of the summit tunnel in one hour.

Dan and Kate climbed into the jeep and drove east on Highway 40 for a short distance, until they could see the cover over the central shaft not far from the highway. They turned right onto a road and drove past a tall white shed, then turned off the road and drove over the rough granite surface to the location of the central shaft.

Dan and Kate walked to the tunnel opening and saw that the eight-by-twelve-foot rectangular shaft opening was covered by a grillwork made from old pear-shaped rail. They looked around the granite surface surrounding the shaft and found the rusted bolts that had once held the *Sacramento* in place alongside the opening. They also found a path that had been cut through the granite to allow the oxen to pull the steam engine into place.

"Kate," said Dan, "it is obvious that the vault must be inside the central shaft. The area around the shaft is solid granite and has never been excavated. We will have to explore the interior of the central shaft to find the vault, and then we will have to figure out how to open it."

Dan and Kate continued searching the area for about thirty minutes, until they saw their archeology students hiking toward them on the old Donner Pass wagon road. Dan and Kate climbed on top of the central shaft cover and waved to them. The students gathered around the shaft, and Dan spoke to them.

"I want to thank you all for your excellent work on this project. Your work has already resulted in many major accomplishments that have written new pages in the history of California. You all know the goal of this project was to validate the pages of Doc Strong's journal and to determine if Judah's gold was really hidden by Doc Strong, Jim Smiley, and Lewis Clement.

"I believe we have found the hiding place of Judah's gold, and it is only a few feet below where I am standing. I hope to get approval from the Southern Pacific Railroad to explore the central shaft of the Summit Tunnel.

"Dr. Kelly and I both believe we will end our quest with the successful discovery of Judah's gold."

There was a sudden outburst of cheering from the students.

Kate then spoke to the students. "It is great to hear your enthusiasm, but we have a lot of work ahead of us. I would like both teams to work together to survey and document the entire area around the summit tunnel central shaft, complete with detailed photographs. I would like you all to remain at the camp or work site and not to contact anyone outside of the project team. We would have every gold seeker in the West interfering with our work, if word were to leak out."

Kate and Dan jumped into the jeep and drove back to the camp near the west portal of the summit tunnel. As they reached the camp, they saw Agents Packard and Chambers waiting for them.

"What's up?" Dan asked.

Packard said, "I am afraid we have bad news for you two. We searched inside the train tunnels and the valley below, and we have found no trace of Veronica Bailey or Bradford Damian. We found the wrecked railroad speeder in the valley below the rail line, but there was no indication that Bailey and Damian flew down the hill with the speeder."

Chambers then said, "We took search teams into the tunnels with searchlights and did not find their bodies. We did find a service opening in the snow shed just east of Tunnel 8 that they could have jumped through from the speeder and would have been safe from the passenger train. We have agents searching the area, but there is a chance they could have flagged down a car on Highway 40 close to China Wall and escaped."

"Damn! That could not have happened at a worse time," said Dan. "We think we have just discovered the gold's hiding place."

"Dan, the news gets worse", said Packard. "We have an agent working undercover as a waiter at the Cal Neva Lodge, observing Sam Giancana's activities, and he told us that there has been a sudden surge in activity at the lodge. There has been an increase in the number of Giancana's men, and he has had a number of closed-door meetings with his lieutenants. Something is about to happen."

"I am sorry, Dan; the Director has instructed us to make Giancana our priority and move all of our agents to the Cal Neva and keep an eye on him. On the positive side, we believe all of Bailey's hired guns are in custody, and she should not be a problem for you in the next few days."

Dan looked at Kate and said, "We will have to finish our work quickly, before Bailey and Damian have time to regroup. Thank you two for all your help, and good luck watching the mob boss."

Packard and Chambers walked off to their car and drove away from the camp, and Dan and Kate walked to a telephone booth at the nearby Donner Ski Ranch. Dan made several telephone calls, and he and Kate waited in the lounge about a half hour for a return call. The payphone rang, and Dan jumped to his feet and answered the call. He spoke on the telephone for a few minutes and then returned to where Kate was sitting.

"Kate, I have good news. The Southern Pacific Railroad has agreed to help us. They had already planned to close the summit tunnel for eight hours tomorrow for track maintenance inside the tunnel. All train traffic will be diverted to Track 2, which travels through the mountain about a mile away from the summit tunnel. They also have agreed to remove the rail grill that covers the central staff and allow us to use a truck-mounted crane to explore the central shaft."

"Will the railroad try to claim the gold?" Kate asked.

"No, Kate. They realize that the gold was paid to Judah, and they have no claim to it. They also realize that it is part of their railroad's history, and they want to have it displayed in a museum for the public to see."

"Let's go get some rest," said Kate, "we have a lot to do before tomorrow morning."

They walked back to their camp and saw a man in work clothes sitting in an orange truck, waiting for them. Dan walked up to the man, who introduced himself to them. He said his name was Jim Roberts, and he was the crew chief for the Southern Pacific crew that would be working in the tunnel.

He told them he had just received a call from the Southern Pacific Headquarters in San Francisco, directing him to do anything he could to help them explore the central shaft of the summit tunnel.

Dan introduced himself and Kate, and then he and Roberts sat at a table and discussed the details of the project for about ten minutes. Dan and Kate got in the truck with Roberts and drove to the central shaft to discuss the placement of the crane for the removal of the rails and exploration of the central shaft. They also discussed how to make a platform that could be lowered into the shaft by the crane. Robertson then drove them back to camp and told them he would meet them at the center shaft at seven o'clock in the morning.

When they reached the camp, Dan and Kate quickly gathered the students. The team leaders told them that they had completed the survey of the area surrounding the central shaft and had documented everything with photographs.

Dan told them to get all of their gear ready to document the opening and exploration of the central shaft, starting at seven o'clock in the morning.

Kate and Dan joined the students for dinner, then went to Kate's tent. Inside the tent, Kate told Dan, "This is really exciting. Just think, by this time tomorrow we may be looking at Judah's gold. We have been talking about finding it since we were kids, and now we have come to the end of our search."

"Yes, we have spent years thinking about the day we would find the gold, but we cannot afford to drop our guard tomorrow. Bailey and Damian are still out there," Dan replied. "Kate, make certain you have your gun tomorrow. It is not likely that Bailey is in a position to interfere, but we have to be prepared. At the first sign of any trouble, I want you to get the students safely away from the site. I have arranged for an armored truck to be ready on the road beside the central shaft to take the gold to a safe place as quickly as possible.

"Good night, Kate. Get some sleep—we have an exciting day ahead of us tomorrow."

CHAPTER TWENTY-THREE

Judah's Gold

Kate peeked into Dan's tent at daybreak, and he was not there. She looked around the camp and saw him walking toward the camp from the direction of the Donner Ski Ranch. When he arrived at the camp, Kate asked him, "What have you been up to?"

Dan told her that he had made some phone calls to make certain everything would go as planned. As they walked to get breakfast, they could see the Southern Pacific maintenance-of-way crew, gathering near the portal of the summit as a west-bound freight train exited the tunnel. Dan said, "That was the last train through the tunnel."

As they ate breakfast they observed the work crew loading equipment onto railroad speeder trailers. They then saw a high-rail truck arrive from the direction of the Norden roundhouse.

"Kate, it looks like they are starting to work inside the tunnel. We'd better get up to the central shaft."

They climbed into a jeep with the two team leaders and made the short drive to the top of the summit tunnel. They walked up to the central shaft, just as the crane truck arrived. Dan guided the crane through the trail that had been cut through the granite in 1866 for the oxen team to haul the *Sacramento* to the central shaft. When the crane truck stopped, Dan noticed that it was being driven by Jim Roberts. Dan walked over to him, and Roberts told him that he would be the crane operator today.

The Southern Pacific crew was in the process of cutting each rail free with an acetylene torch. When all the rails were removed, they attached the work platform to four guide cables, which they then attached to the hook at the end of the crane's cable. Roberts carefully lifted the platform, placed it in position in the shaft opening, and said, "Dr. Strong, it is time for you to climb onboard."

Dan and Kate climbed on the platform, carrying spotlights and a camera. Dan used a hand radio to tell Roberts to lower them four feet into the shaft. They turned on their spotlights as soon as the platform started descending. They both looked carefully at the walls of the shaft and saw a roughly carved granite surface with a deep layer of soot covering it. Kate said, "This surface is black as coal, and it is going to be very difficult to find anything. Exactly what are we looking for, Dan?"

"Let me know if you see or feel anything unusual on the surface of the walls. The clue in Smiley's gold watch was engraved with a compass with an arrow pointing east."

As they searched, they ran their hands over the walls and discovered a few circular holes left that remained from the black powder blasting. The holes seemed random, so Dan radioed

Roberts to lower them another four feet. They repeated this process until they reached the twenty-foot level. When they searched this level, Dan found a series of holes placed close together. He turned the spotlight on them and said, "They would never have drilled holes that close together for blasting, and the outside holes form the directions of the compass. There are also two holes inside the compass coordinates. There is a large hole in the center and another triangular hole pointing to the north hole of the compass."

"I wonder...." Dan mused.

"Take a photograph of this, Kate."

After the camera flashed, Dan took the two artifacts out of his jacket and placed the triangular end of the metal spike into the triangular hole pointed North. He then placed Judah's surveyor's plum bob into the large center hole, and they hear a loud thud sound inside the granite wall. He pushed on the granite wall and nothing happened. He looked at the compass hole again said, "I think I know the rest of the combination to this vault. Smiley's watch has an arrow pointing east, and this triangular hole is pointing north...let me try something."

Dan then put the metal spike in the hole and pulled it toward the East hole. Slowly he felt the granite inside the compass move in a circular direction until it stopped with the triangular arrow hole pointed to the east. Suddenly there was another thud, and a ten-foot section of the granite wall pivoted in the center, exposing a vault chamber.

Kate pointed the searchlight into the vault and saw a ten-by-eight-foot chamber with twelve wooden barrels stacked inside. Kate shouted, "We found it, Dan!"

She quickly took a photo of the interior of the vault and they both jumped from the platform into the vault. They used their flashlights to carefully examine the vault and the old wooden barrels. Dan said, "The barrels appear to be in excellent shape, considering they have been here for almost one hundred years."

Dan directed his spotlight at the walls of the vault and saw that the entire inside area had been coated with a tar-like substance, which had waterproofed the vault. He looked at Kate and said, "Lewis Clement's crew of Chinese workers did an amazing job cutting this vault from granite as hard as steel and then sealing it from the harsh Sierra storms. The truly amazing thing is, the vault door that opened like a puzzle and was totally invisible to anyone searching for it."

"I know I should wait until the contents of the vault are photographed and cataloged, but I am going to open one of the barrels." Kate quickly took a series of photographs showing the location of each barrel. Dan looked at all of the barrels and noticed that four of the barrels were a different size than the others. He walked up to one of these barrels and carefully used his knife to remove the top. When he lifted the lid, he could see a canvas bag. Kate pointed her spotlight at the bag, and when Dan opened the bag, they could see the brilliant reflection of gold coins. Dan took one of the coins out and it was a 1855 fifty-dollar golden eagle—a twin to the coin that had been passed down to him from Doc Strong.

"We have done it, Kate! We have found Judah's gold!"

CHAPTER TWENTY-FOUR

Veronica's Gold

Dan and Kate turned around in the vault and discovered that the platform was no longer outside the vault. Dan used his radio to call Roberts. "Jim, what happened to the platform?"

Roberts replied that he would send the platform back down to them. "I wonder what is going on," said Dan.

A few minutes later, Dan and Kate saw the platform arrive in front of the vault opening. Standing on the platform were Veronica Bailey, her bodyguard, and Bradford Damian. The guard pointed a pistol at Dan, and Bailey said, "Thank you for doing all the hard work and finding the gold for me. Too bad you didn't accept my partnership arrangement. Now all of the gold belongs to me." Veronica then looked into the open barrel and smiled as she said, "The gold coins are even more beautiful than I imagined."

The guard gestured with his gun for Kate and Dan to get on the platform. Bailey jumped back onto the platform after Dan and Kate. Damian frisked Dan and took his gun. He then radi-oed to bring the platform to the surface, and it started to move immediately. When they reached the surface, they could see all the students sitting in a group, and a man with a machine gun was standing over them. Dan recognized him instantly. He was the man, who had been his guard at the Cal Neva Lodge. Bailey said, "Your students will not be harmed if you cooperate with me. As you can see, I have gotten some help from Jim."

Dan looked up at a smiling Jim Roberts as he sat at the con-trols of the crane, and Bailey said, "It is amazing what money can buy. Mr. Roberts was also responsible for sabotaging the tracks when we went to China Wall. He contacted me when he found out that you would be exploring the central shaft of the summit tunnel."

Dan stared at Bailey and told her she would never get the gold out. "Highway 40 is the only way down from Donner Pass, and the FBI will catch you before you can reach Soda Springs or Truckee."

Bailey grinned as she said, " I don't plan on traveling by road."

She looked at the central shaft and said, "The opening of that shaft is about seventy-five feet above the Southern Pacific railroad tracks in the tunnel. The crane will lower the gold to several railroad speeders with trailers below the shaft. Because of the maintenance work, there will not be any trains on that track for at least another seven hours. That will give me plenty of time to get to a remote location, safe from the FBI."

Bailey told them it was time to go, and that Dan and Kate would supervise the loading of the barrels. Bailey and the guard climbed onto the platform, and Damian told Kate and Dan to get back on the platform. The crane lowered them to the vault, and Damian, Kate, and Dan entered the granite vault. Dan and Damian rolled four barrels onto the platform, and it was lowered to the tunnel below.

Bailey watched the barrels being loaded onto the small rail cars trailing the speeders. The platform was returned to the vault, and four more barrels were loaded onto the trailers. The platform then returned for the last four barrels. When the barrels were loaded, Damian jumped on to the platform and told Dan and Kate to stay inside the vault. He then pushed on the granite door of the vault, and it pivoted shut. As the door closed, Damian shouted, "Goodbye, Dr. Strong, maybe they will find your bones a hundred years from now!"

As the granite door closed, Dan used his spotlight to block the locking bolt and pushed the door open. Kate looked at Dan and said, "How are we going to get out of here? It is too far to jump and impossible to climb out."

"Kate, I have an idea," said Dan. He explained that the workers would have to raise the platform out of the shaft, and they could jump onto it as it passed by the entrance to the vault. He asked Kate if she still had her gun, and she said, "Yes—I can't believe they didn't search me."

Kate handed the gun to Dan, and they noticed that the cable for the platform was moving. Kate pointed her spotlight down the cable, and they could see that Bailey's men had removed the platform from the hook at the end of the cable.

Dan gave Kate a kiss and said, "I will be right back, sweetheart."

He then jumped out of the vault and held on to the cable hook. When he reached the surface he swung on the cable and rolled out onto ground. He pulled the gun out of his waistband and fired two shots at the man with the machine gun. The man groaned and hit the ground.

Dan pointed the gun at Roberts, and he raised his hands and came down from the crane. Dan tied Roberts hands with a rope, and gave the pistol to one of the students and told him to watch the two men. He then asked if any of the students knew how to operate the crane. One of the students jumped up and told him he had used a crane just like this one in Columbia.

Dan then told the rest of the students to head back to camp to call Special Agent Packard and tell him what happened—and that Veronica Bailey was escaping by rail from the summit tunnel.

Dan then took another platform from the back of the crane truck and attached it to the crane's cable hook. He picked up the Thompson machine gun and jumped onto the platform as it was lowered to the vault. Kate jumped onto the platform and hugged him tightly as the platform was lowered down to the tunnel. Just before they reached the railroad tunnel, Dan told Kate to lie flat on the platform in case someone shot at them.

Dan could see Bailey was gone when the platform reached the track. He and Kate got off the platform, and Dan radioed the crane operator to raise the platform out of the shaft.

Kate asked, "Which direction did Bailey go?"

Dan told her that Bailey was too smart to head east. "If she went east, she would be too exposed during the long trip through Cold Stream Canyon and Stanford's Curve. She must have gone west. She would be going downhill, and after she passes Norden and Soda Springs, there are very few places where she could be caught."

Dan noticed an orange high-rail truck that had been left at the entrance to the summit tunnel. He and Kate quickly hiked out of the tunnel and climbed into the truck.

Dan drove the truck onto the rails and pulled a lever that lowered front and rear railroad wheels onto the track. He then shifted the truck into gear and headed west toward the Norden snow shed. As they drove, Dan turned on the truck's two-way radio and dialed the frequency that Packard's agents used. Dan reached Packard and Chambers just as he exited the Norden shed.

He explained what had happened and told them that Bailey and the gold were headed west on Track 1.

Packard told Dan that his agents would try to intercept Bailey from the tracks downhill. Dan told him that Bailey had a head start and was moving down the rail at a fast rate of speed. He estimated that Bailey's speeders had already passed Yuba Gap.

Dan told Packard that if his men hurried, they would be able to trap Bailey when she reached Blue Canyon. He explained that the tracks made a huge arc through the canyon, and if they were to intercept them in the canyon, Bailey would be unable to escape, because agents could block the only road out of the canyon. Dan said he and Kate would continue to follow Bailey to make certain she did not escape before she reached Blue Canyon.

Dan and Kate's high-rail truck arrived at the station in Blue Canyon and stopped at the old station building when they saw Packard and Chambers standing near the track. Packard said, "My men saw Bailey escape through the tunnel at the end of the canyon before they could reach the track. I have sent men to Gold Run and Colfax to try to intercept them."

Dan said, "We will continue to follow Bailey to make sure she does not escape at some point before there."

Packard's radio made a static sound, and one of his men reported that the Highway Patrol had seen the speeders traveling through Gold Run and Alta.

Dan looked at Packard and said, "You should also send some men to Bowman at the point where Track 1 and Track 2 separate. If she gets past that point, she will have many ways to escape when she reaches Auburn."

Dan stepped on the gas pedal, and the high-rail truck sped off and exited the canyon through the tunnel. About an hour later, an agent reported that Bailey's speeders were seen crossing the Long Ravine Trestle and speeding through Colfax just before they had arrived to block the track.

Dan picked up the microphone and told Packard that he and Kate were about to cross the trestle at Colfax. They had closed the gap and were only a few minutes behind Bailey. He asked him to have some armed agents board his truck when he reached Colfax. Dan stopped the high-rail truck near a fruit shed in Colfax, and three agents jumped into the back of the truck. He sped off as soon as the agents were onboard. Dan knew they were only a few minutes behind Bailey, and they would most likely catch up to her before she reached Bowman.

The truck sped by Applegate and Clipper Gap and arrived at Bowman without catching Bailey.

"Where the hell did she go?" asked Dan, when he saw Packard and Chambers standing on the track in front of him.

Packard told Dan that there is no way Bailey could have gotten past this point. His men were already here when she was reported passing Colfax. Dan told Packard they did not see any sign of Bailey or her speeders—it was like she had disappeared into thin air. Kate said, "It is just like a magician made her disappear."

Dan said, "Magicians use illusion to perform their magic. Bailey used some sort illusion or trick to avoid being seen, and I think I know what she did."

Dan explained that between Applegate and Clipper Gap, the railroad had built Tunnel Zero on Track 1. "During World War II, they discovered the tunnel was too small for trains to move landing craft through, and they bypassed it. Tunnel Zero is now hidden by overgrowth between Track 1 and Tunnel 23 on the eastbound track. There are railroad maintenance workers with her, and they would know the location of the tunnel. Bailey must have hidden in the abandoned tunnel with the speeders and all the gold."

Packard told Dan that he would take half of his men and follow the tracks toward Tunnel Zero from the east, and Chambers would approach the tunnel from the west.

Dan drove the speeder off the rails, then reversed his direction and drove back onto the track and said, "Kate, you better jump off here. Things are going to be extremely dangerous when we corner Bailey."

"No way am I going to miss seeing Bailey's capture," Kate protested. "I am staying with you, Dan."

Dan knew it would be useless to argue, so he stepped on the gas and accelerated the truck back toward Tunnel Zero. A few minutes later, they passed Clipper Gap, and Dan slowed down when he saw Tunnel 23 above and to the left of Track 1. Just below this tunnel, he could see the leaves of a tree covering the west portal of Tunnel Zero.

He stopped the truck when he was near the tree and radioed Packard and Chambers that he had reached Tunnel Zero. Chambers responded that his men had found the eastern portal of the tunnel and were in position.

Packard reported that he could see Dan about one hundred yards ahead of him and said, "We will coordinate our assault on the tunnel from both ends."

Dan clicked the radio transmit button and said, "I will try to approach the tunnel from the west side and get a peek inside and report what I see."

Dan carefully approached the tunnel opening from the side and reported he could not see any guards at the entrance. He looked inside the tunnel and found himself face to face with Veronica Bailey. She took a step out of the tunnel with a gun pointed at him.

"Veronica, you will not get away this time. There are agents at both ends of this tunnel, and there is no way you can escape."

Veronica moved the gun to Dan's head and said, "I will take you hostage, and you will be my ticket out here, Dr. Strong."

Suddenly, there was a gunshot, and a bullet struck Bailey on her arm, causing her gun to fall to the ground.

"Not this time, bitch", said Kate, standing in the entrance of the tunnel with a gun in her hand. "It is all over for you, Veronica. I hope you like your new accommodations in prison."

Packard and Chambers' men attacked both sides of the tunnel when they heard the gunshot, and all of Bailey's men dropped their guns and surrendered. Packard arrived and handcuffed a bandaged Bailey to the truck.

Kate and Dan walked into the tunnel and found all twelve barrels. They looked into the open barrel and untied the canvas bag. Inside, the bag of gold coins glistened in the light from the tunnel portal.

"We've done it, Dan. After all these years of research, we know the truth about the history of California's first transcontinental railroad and the men that built it."

As they walked out of the tunnel, Dan kissed Kate and said, "By the way, Kate, thanks for taking care of Bailey and saving my butt."

Kate smiled mischievously and said, "My pleasure, sweetheart. Bailey has been interfering with my wedding plans for far too long."

CHAPTER TWENTY-FIVE

End of the Quest

Six Months Later at Stanford University Library

Kate and Dan walked through the entrance of the Stanford University Library and were immediately surrounded by the familiar faces of their graduate students and friends.

Kate had decided the library was the perfect place to have their wedding reception. As they walked into the main room, they could see the Central Pacific Railroad locomotive, the *Governor Stanford*, surrounded by exhibit cases full of Judah's gold coins.

Special Agents Packard, Chambers, and Sperry were standing near the exhibit cases, and they each gave Kate a big hug and kiss. Kate smiled and said, "It is wonderful to see you all again. Without your help, there would not have been a wedding or this wonderful exhibit." Dan shook their hands, and they all walked closer to the exhibit. The *Governor Stanford* locomotive was the first steam locomotive to run on the Central Pacific Railroad, and it was a fitting centerpiece to be surrounded by glass exhibit cases displaying all 2,000 of Theodore Judah's fifty-dollar gold coins.

The exhibit also displayed the miners' barrels of gold and the huge Carson Hill nugget that had been rescued from Veronica Bailey's trophy room at the top of the Chrysler building.

Packard looked around the building and noticed numerous armed guards conspicuously stationed around the library. He said, "I see you are taking no chances and protecting Judah's gold, even though Veronica Bailey is securely locked away in a high-security prison for the next century."

"Yes, but our friend Bradford Damian somehow managed to escape again and he is an extremely intelligent and dangerous black-market thief who always manages to show up when you least expect him."

Chamber's looked at the gold coins and asked Dan, "What will you do with all of Judah's gold after this exhibit?"

"We will lock it away in Stanford University's vault, until a suitable site for its permanent display can be found. Kate and I hope that a Museum of Railroad History can be built to commemorate the fulfillment of Theodore Judah's dream of building the first transcontinental railroad. We believe the perfect site for this museum would be on the Sacramento waterfront, where the first track was laid for the Central Pacific Railroad."

One of Kate and Dan's graduate students walked up to them with a white wedding gift box and said, "This present just arrived, and I thought you might want to see it right away. The present is from Bradford Damian."

Dan and Kate immediately looked at each other in total surprise. Packard and Sperry took the present to a nearby table, and Packard said, "If you don't mind, we had better be careful and look this over before it is opened."

They carefully examined the package and removed the wrapping paper. They then lifted the lid, exposing white tissue paper. They removed the tissue paper and exposed a beautiful, jeweled Roman sword and gold scabbard.

"Oh, my God! It is the sword of Tiberius Caesar!" said Kate

Dan lifted the sword and could see it had a gold and jewel-encrusted handle and pommel cap. He then looked carefully at the engraving on the gold scabbard and said, "There is a sword and scabbard similar to this made of bronze in the British Museum. It was presented to one of Tiberius' senior officers. I have never heard of one made of gold. This was Tiberius Caesar's personal sword."

"Damian must have looted it from our dig at the Villa Jovis without us knowing about it," Kate said. She picked up a card inside the box and read a note from Damian.

"Best wishes to my favorite archeologists on your wedding day. I hope you enjoy your gift. I look forward to seeing you on your next project.

-Bradford Damian, Esq."

Packard asked Kate and Dan, "Where will you be going next?"

Kate smiled at Dan and said, "We will honeymoon in the Tuscan hills, and archeology will be last thing on our minds."

Dan and Kate then waved at everyone in the room, ran to Kate's red Thunderbird outside the door, and made their escape.

ABOUT THE AUTHOR

Ralph Orlandella is a native Californian, born and raised in Lodi, California. He was exposed to railroading and California history at a very young age. His father and uncle owned a produce-packing company in Lodi, and Ralph would frequently visit their fruit-packing shed and watch as blocks of railroad refrigerator cars were loaded for shipment to east coast markets. He witnessed the railroad's transition from steam locomotives to diesel electric locomotives. Lodi is located as a gateway to California's "gold country," and Ralph's family would take frequent trips up to the Mother Lode counties. Ralph was impressed the area's rich history.

Ralph received a bachelor's degree and doctorate in pharmacy from the University of the Pacific. During his college days, he was fortunate to have the opportunity to study California history under historian Dr. R. Coke Wood, named "Mr. California" by the California legislature. Ralph's professional career included working as a director of pharmacy, a hospital administrator, and a pharmacy inspector for the California State Board of Pharmacy, where his investigations brought him to all four corners of the state.

His railroad experience includes a decade as the president of the volunteer docent council at the California State Railroad Museum. There he helped found the museum's very successful Sacramento Southern Railroad, which provides steam railroad excursions from Old Sacramento State Park. He also helped develop the museum's Amtrak Interpretive Program, which daily provides narrators on Amtrak's *California Zephyr* on the Sierra Nevada Mountain's Donner Pass route, between Sacramento and Reno. Ralph also has served as the executive director of the California State Railroad Museum Foundation and has owned and operated private passenger railcars across the United States.

Ralph has combined all of his experience to write *Search For Judah's Gold* and has interwoven a fictional adventure story line with real events and actual places that were part of Theodore Judah's dream—the building of the first transcontinental railroad.

Made in the USA
Charleston, SC
30 January 2012